ANNIE M.P. SMITHSON (1873-1948) was the most successful of all Irish romantic novelists. Her nineteen books, including Nora Connor, Paid in Full, The Walk of a Queen, Her Irish Heritage, *and* The Marriage of Nurse Harding *were all bestsellers, with their wholesome mix of old-fashioned romance, spirited characters and commonsense philosophy.*

She was born in Sandymount, Co. Dublin, and reared in the strict Unionist tradition. On completion of her training as a nurse in London and Edinburgh, she returned to Dublin and was posted north as a Queen's Nurse in 1901. Here, for the first time, she experienced the divide between Irish Nationalists and Unionists, and it appalled her. She converted to Catholicism at the age of 34 and was subsequently disowned by most of her family. She immersed herself in the Republican movement — actively canvassing for Sinn Féin in the 1918 General Election, nursing Dubliners during the influenza epidemic of that year, instructing Cumann na mBan on nursing care and tending the wounded of the Civil War in 1922. She was arrested and imprisoned, and threatened to go on hunger-strike unless released.

Forced to resign her commission in the strongly Loyalist Queen's Nurses Committee, she took up private work and tended the poor of Dublin city until she retired in 1942. During her long career, she did much to improve the lot of the nursing profession and championed its cause as Secretary of the Irish Nurses Union.

In later years, she devoted herself to her writing and was an active member of WAAMA, PEN and the Old Dublin Socity, Her autobiography, Myself — and Others, was completed in 1944, four years before her death at the age of 75.

NORA CONNOR

by

ANNIE M.P. SMITHSON

THE MERCIER PRESS

THE MERCIER PRESS, Cork

First published by The Talbot Press

This edition 1990
(c) The Mercier Press, 1989

ISBN 978 1 78117 925 3
Transferred to Digital Print-on-Demand in 2024

1

THE RISE OF THE CURTAIN

From the moment the curtain rose Nora Connor's eyes were fixed on the stage. She sat entranced, as countless other people have been, and will be to the end of time, by the fascinating realism and matchless imagery of the Bard of Avon.

It was a matinee of *Romeo and Juliet*, and, filling the title roles were the incomparable actor and actress who in the last decade of the nineteenth century excelled all the other great tragedians of Shakespearian history. Never, in all their own triumphant experience had the fame of these two superb artists drawn together a more enthusiastic audience than that which witnessed their performance that day in the Gaiety Theatre, Dublin.

Nora sat beside her mother. Those of us who are old enough will remember that in the nineties of the last century girls did not go to the theatre unchaperoned. The day of the 'flapper' was not yet, and the code of etiquette for the unmarried girl was very different in many respects from what it is today. Nora, sitting demurely beside stout Mrs Connor, was as unlike the young girl of our period in thought, word, and deed, as she was in dress.

Picture her to yourself, dear reader, in long skirt and leg-of-mutton sleeve, with queerly shaped hat, and hair done in fringe and 'bun'. What dowdy, unbecoming fashions they would seem to us now! What states of astonishment, what smiles of derision would follow such a figure if it were seen walking down Grafton Street in our time! But Nora of 1899 was quite pleased with herself, and well she might be, for, according to the vogue of that day, she was suitably and fashionably attired. Very pretty she was, too, although looking much older than a girl of her age would look in the dress and make-up of the present time.

It was her first time seeing *Romeo and Juliet* acted, but she knew the play by heart, and so sat, as we have said, entranced, and oblivious of all around her, until the curtain fell on the first act. Only then, as the lights went up, did she turn to her mother and express her delight.

Mrs Connor, middle-aged and stout, the wife of a successful grocer, and a lady passionately ambitious of obtaining admission into society, smiled indulgently.

'Very nice, very pretty, indeed, my dear,' she said. 'I am glad you are enjoying yourself.'

As for the good lady herself, a pantomime or music hall 'turn' would have been of equal merit in her eyes. It was the 'correct' thing to 'do' a matinee now and then, especially if one had a young daughter; and Mrs Connor was particularly glad that she had come this afternoon, as her friends, Lady Dempsey, the wife of a publican knight, and Mrs Malone, who 'went to the castle', were both seated near her in the dress circle. She was nodding pleasantly to them now, and leaning towards them to exchange remarks; and thus her daughter, having made her polite duty bow to her elders, found herself at liberty to look round at the audience.

Seated just behind her, a little to the right, was a young man who had been looking at her with evident interest. Becoming conscious of his scrutiny, Nora turned her head slightly and met his gaze.

He was about eight and twenty, with reddish-brown hair and a keen intellectual face. Two things she noticed about him were out of the ordinary. He allowed a little of his hair to grow down each side of his face in front of the ears, which gave him a foreign appearance; and his eyes, which, like the hair, were reddish-brown, would flame red in moments of excitement. They were red now, as they looked into the soft grey eyes of Nora Connor for a moment, ere, flushing vividly, she turned away. But she found herself still thinking of him, after the curtain had gone up; and in the handsome features of the love-sick Romeo she seemed to see again the face of the man in the seat behind. During the second interval she did not dare to glance round, but sat gazing demurely in front of her at nothing in particular, perfectly conscious, however, that the pair of red-brown eyes behind were fixed intently upon her.

But the strange fates that shape the course of human destiny had decreed that she and Duke Percival were to meet each other that day. After a while, during a pause in her 'society' chatter with Mrs Connor, Lady Dempsey, glancing round, caught sight of the young man. She had been introduced to him at some viceregal function to which many of the minor society people had received invitations. Doubtless he had since forgotten even her very existence, but she felt there was now a golden opportunity presented to her of renewing the acquaintance. For Duke Percival was worth knowing. He was one of those whose help counted when one was trying to climb the rungs of the social ladder and finding it rather a difficult feat.

So Lady Dempsey, having managed to attract his attention, said archly:'Why, I declare, if it's not Mr Percival! How charming to meet you again!'

Now, it is more than probable that had Mr Percival not noticed that Lady Dempsey and Mrs Connor were fraternising, the lady's very cordial recognition might have been but coldly received. As it was he replied with equal warmth: 'Lady Dempsey! How good of you to remember me! I cannot tell you what a pleasure it is to see you again!'

He had a really beautiful voice — a voice that was a most valuable asset to him in his profession. Many of his brother barristers envied him his voice, which had been known to move juries to tears and sometimes to soften the heart of the hardest judge on the bench. He used it to good effect now, so that Lady Dempsey actually blushed with pleasure as she replied to his flattery.

And then came his reward — the goal to which he had played.

'Mrs Connor, may I introduce my friend, Mr Duke Percival? Mrs Connor — Miss Connor.'

It was done, and, like most of the things that really matter in our lives, it was done in a few seconds.

Lady Dempsey and Mrs Malone were in the seats in front of Mrs Connor, and thus the three ladies could converse at ease and, indeed, confidentially. Nora was nearest to Duke Percival. She had only to turn slightly to be able to talk to him as if he were sitting beside her. Needless to remark, he helped her by leaning forward and listening to her with an eagerness about which there was no pretence. He found himself watching with secret delight her quick vivid blushes and the shy glances which she threw at him from time to time as he discussed the play and the acting. But he was intensely amused when, on his venturing to criticise some part, she broke out impatiently: 'Oh! don't say that. I think it is all so perfect. And I want to think of it as a real thing. To me they are all alive. I forget it is only a play.' The red-brown eyes smiled at her in frank amusement.

'Then is this the first time you have seen it?' he asked.

'Oh, yes — the very first,' she replied. 'I have never seen a real play before—only the pantomimes and Hengler's circus. We had theatricals at school, but the nuns would not allow us to play *Romeo and Juliet.* We had other kinds of plays, very good and religious, but I think now that they were dreadfully dull.'

'You must make up for lost time,' he said. 'I suppose you will be often at the theatre in future.'

'Oh, I don't know! Mamma thinks that girls should not go too often. And then I have only just left school, and she keeps me almost like a schoolgirl still.'

He smiled inwardly at the pretty petulance of her tone, and the childish 'Mamma'.

'Oh, that's too bad,' he replied, his voice dangerously soft. 'We must try to persuade her to be less stern, now that you are a young lady.'

She met his smiling glance, and then, as he laughed, she laughed back again. When one is eighteen, and has just left school routine and regulations behind, the world seems a pleasant place indeed, with almost unlimited possibilities for happiness. One learns a different lesson soon enough; and Nora Connor was to discover by her own experience in the days to come what so many had discovered before her, that the happiness of girlhood is a fleeting thing.

But while Duke Percival and Nora are smiling and laughing together, let us listen awhile to the elder ladies, who are also engaged in animated conversation.

'I am really surprised that you have not heard of him,' Lady Dempsey was saying, in reply to a remark made by Mrs Malone. 'He is one of the Percivals of Meath—a very old family — Anglo-Normans, you know. They have a beautiful estate at Belmont, their place in County Meath, and a town house in Fitzwilliam Square. He is the second son, and is making a name for himself at the bar. The elder, Everard , is the heir, and lives at Belmont with the old people. He cares only for country life — hunting and the like. A complete contrast to dear Duke, who is of quite a literary turn of mind.'

What 'dear Duke', would have thought could he have heard his family and personal character thus discussed by a woman he had met only once before in his life, may be better left to the imagination. But, at the moment, he was oblivious of everybody save the girl to whom he was talking.

Lady Dempsey's friends listened with avidity. Although their money and 'push' did much for them in the society of the Irish capital of that period, still they knew perfectly well that by the really good families they would never be 'received'. But they clung to the hope that perhaps some day —. And now, here was the opportunity itself, in the person of this young man, who represented one of the 'County Families'. How providential!

Mrs Connor especially was charmed. She glanced behind and saw him as, leaning forward, he talked to Nora. And he seemed deeply interested, she thought. What a splendid match for the dear girl! But he was a second son, Lady Dempsey had said. Mrs Connor turned to her friend for more definite information.

'Of course, I have often heard of the Percivals of Meath,' she said, 'a fine old family. But I always understood that they were not rich — at least, not for their position. So I suppose, as your Mr Percival is the second son, he has to try to make a fortune as well as a name for himself in his profession?'

'Oh, no,' was the reply. 'He is one of the lucky ones of the earth. His godmother, old Mrs Vandeleur, left him a comfortable fortune. He need not practise at the bar to make money. But he is very ambitious.'

All this was intensely satisfactory. Mrs Connor stole a glance behind. She had moved into a vacant seat beside her friends during the interval, and she now saw the two young people still engrossed in conversation with each other and oblivious of all around them.

'He is not — eh — of course, a Catholic?' she ventured, hesitating a little in asking the question, for fear Lady Dempsey or Mrs Malone, both of whom she feared somewhat and indeed rather disliked, would follow the trend of her thoughts.

'A Catholic!' echoed Lady Dempsey. 'Good gracious, no! Why the man is quite unorthodox in his views. He is not a professing Christian of any sort.'

Mrs Connor gasped with horror, and Mrs.Malone, glancing at her with a malicious smile, observed nastily: 'Not a very suitable match for a Catholic girl, Mrs Connor, even if he felt inclined that way, or —'

She did not finish the sentence, but threw a contemptuous glance at the youthful pair behind. Mrs Connor flushed crimson, and, leaving her friends rather abruptly, went back to her own seat, beside Nora. She answered coldly when Duke spoke to her, and felt relieved when the curtain went up and Nora had turned her whole attention once more to the stage.

When the play was over they left the theatre together, mother and daughter, the young man who had been so charming helping them with wraps and coats in the easy well-bred manner, so delightful to middle-class women, whose husbands never think of such acts of courtesy. Mrs Connor, finding it impossible to remain stiff any longer, smiled and talked to the young man in her friendliest manner.

But Nora was silent — the silence of perfect bliss, of an almost unbelievable happiness. That she should have been to her first Shakespearian play, and have met *him* on the same day!

It seemed too wonderful to be true.

'You must come and see us, Mr Percival,' she heard her mother say, as that good lady extended a fat hand which was like to burst its tight kid glove. 'I am at home every second Wednesday. Now, don't forget.'

'Thank you so much. It will be a pleasure,' was the reply; and he bowed over that formidable hand as though it had been the hand of royalty itself.

Then he turned to Nora. She was drawing her wrap round her with pretty, slender fingers, over which she had not yet drawn her gloves. Could such as she be the daughter of that stout, vulgar woman? To Duke Percival it was amazing, incredible. He held her hand a little longer than was usual — continued to hold it, even under the lynx-like glances of the elder ladies. It was so delightful to see the quick, warm blushes, to feel the trembling of the imprisoned fingers.

Lady Dempsey's carriage was waiting, and she graciously asked Mrs Connor to share it with her as their homeward road was the same. A moment later saw Percival bowing his adieu with the strange old-world charm which seemed so natural to him, and saw the ladies smiling and nodding graciously in return. But as they drove off Duke saw only a little hand, yet ungloved, that waved to him for a moment at the window as the carriage drove away.

2

DUKE PERCIVAL AT HOME

In Dublin today most of us who are unmarried and workers live in flats—when we can get them. But in the nineties there were comparatively few women workers. The army of women now so formidable who go daily to their work in offices, banks or business concerns, was a very small army twenty-six years ago. Even if a woman had to work for her living in one of these positions then she either stayed in her own home with her parents, or, if that was not possible, went to a boarding-house as a paying guest. The idea of a young woman living alone in a flat would have met with rigid disapproval from Mrs Grundy — who at that period was still a power in the land. With men, of course, it was different. Man then considered himself the lord of creation, and indeed was still so regarded by many women, who were only beginning in a feeble way to revolt against the shackles of convention that had enslaved their sex for so long. No restraint was put on masculine action, so that if a young fellow with money and leisure chose to install himself in a town flat rather than live under the parental roof-tree, he was at perfect liberty to do so.

And Duke Percival, barrister-at-law, 'of quite a literary turn of mind', according to Lady Dempsey, and ultra-modern in all his ideas, had a very charming bachelor flat near Fitzwilliam Street. Not only was it charming but it also contained much that was uncommon, for its owner had travelled a good deal and had brought back souvenirs from many lands. There were hand-woven carpets and quaint rugs on the floors; curtains of silken brocade at the windows; and the walls were in many places covered with such tapestry as would have turned a collector green with envy. The furniture was mostly antique, for Percival was a good deal of a connoisseur. Many an article had a history of its own, too, and queer tales could be told of how he had acquired them in different lands and at different times.

He loved his flat, and took almost a woman's interest in it; for, like many men who possess the artistic temperament, he had a strong strain of feminism in his character. He always regarded No. 29, Andover Mansions as his real home, and a visit to his family at Belmont was rather in the nature of a penance which he felt called upon to undergo at stated periods. He detested life as lived in the country parts of Ireland. He had often been in the isolated regions of the earth, and had enjoyed the lonely grandeur with which he had been surrounded; but the narrow-minded provincialism of Irish country life filled him with disgust. Every day that he passed in the atmosphere of Belmont was a day of trial and strain upon his patience.

His servant was a Frenchman, whom he had brought with him to Ireland five years before, after a walking tour which he and his friend Jack Vane had made in the districts south of Paris. Pierre Lamont was devoted to his master, and served him with a dog-like fidelity that caused many of Duke's acquaintances to declare that there must be some reason for it — some hidden tale which Percival could unfold—'if he would'. But Percival was dumb on the subject; as was also his friend Vane, who presumably shared his confidence in this as in all other matters.

After the theatre Duke went for a sharp walk to try to chase from his mind, if possible, all thought of the events of the evening. It seemed so absurd that he — a man of the world who had met and known women of every class and type, and who had loved not a few — should have been knocked over by a pair of innocent eyes and a babyish smile. It was incredible-ridiculous!

He arrived at his flat shortly after seven o'clock, and when he stepped into his charming hallway, Pierre was at his side immediately.

'Monsieur is late,' he murmured, as he took his master's hat and coat. 'Monsieur has had tea?'

'Yes — no — it does not matter! I will wait for dinner.'

'I will hurry it for Monsieur.' Pierre was cook as well as valet, with a boy to help him in the kitchen.

'There is no need; I'm not hungry.'

He was turning to ascend the stairs when Pierre spoke again: 'Monsieur Vane telephoned to say that he would be here at a quarter to eight. Monsieur will wait for him?'

'Oh! of course — dinner in half an hour, then.' But his face was frowning as he turned stairwards.

Pierre looked after him for a moment in some surprise. What had happened to Monsieur that he looked so unlike himself? Then the faithful valet hurried to the kitchen regions to hasten up his assistant, who was an extremely lazy fellow.

In the meanwhile Duke had a bath, and then changed, having found all his things laid out as usual with scrupulous care by his valet's deft hands.

Just as he had finished dressing he heard the door bell ring, and guessed that it was Jack Vane arriving. Going down without delay to the library he found his friend standing on the rug before the cheery fire.

The library was lined from floor to ceiling on three sides with books. On the other wall were hung a couple of good pictures; a few comfortable real men's chairs were scattered about; a soft-hued Persian carpet covered the floor; and there was a wide oaken bureau, and a queer gate-legged table. Books and papers were everywhere, and a general air of comfort and untidiness — as well as a pleasant aroma of good tobacco — permeated the room. Over the fireplace hung a good copy of the ever inscrutable and intriguing 'Mona Lisa', and on the mantelpiece itself were great jars of fragrant tobacco, with quaintly designed pipe racks at the side.

Duke's friend was an older man than himself, being a couple of years over thirty. He was not so tall as Percival, and was much slighter; darker, too, with hair that was almost black and well brushed away from his forehead. His eyes were dark brown, and he wore a light moustache. By some he was considered the better looking of the two men, and perhaps, judged by the ordinary standard of masculine good looks, he might have been so; but Duke was of a more uncommon and distinguished type, and in physique, too, he was greatly Jack's superior.

From boyhood they had been 'pals' in the best sense of the word, and there was now a glad look on both their faces which told of the regard each still felt for the other. They had time for only a few commonplace remarks before the admirable Pierre announced that dinner was served. Duke thrust his arm affectionately through Jack's and they crossed the corridor to the dining-room.

The arranging and fitting-up of this room had been a source of undiluted pleasure to Duke, and he had certainly every reason to feel pleased at the finished effect. The walls were done in dark oak panelling: the floor, too, was polished oak, with only a few rugs scattered over its shining surface. A real Jacobean dresser stood against the wall, and the table and chairs were of the same period. Candles were the only light, but there were plenty of these — candles of purest wax, burning in the great silver candelabra, and in queer old brass holders. The appointments of the dinner-table were perfect: the old Waterford glass, the rat-tailed silver, the Indian finger bowls, the chrysanthemums in their quaint vases — all made a picture that was very charming. Excellent, too, was the dinner itself, for Pierre as a chef had few equals.

To Jack Vane, who had no private income of his own, but depended on his work as a journalist and writer of stories to keep him in bread and butter, his friend's mode of living seemed luxurious indeed. Vane was enjoying his dinner with the zest of one who does not get such food every day, but he was quick to observe that Duke was only pretending to eat. In vain Pierre hovered solicitously about his chair, tempting him with various dishes.

'What's up, old man?' asked Vane presently. 'Feeling seedy?'

'Seedy? No, I'm all right,' replied the other, rousing himself with an effort. 'Just a bit tired, I think.'

'Tired? What were you doing this evening?'

'Gaiety matinee, and — a walk afterwards.'

'And that tired you?' laughed the other. 'By Jove! I wish you had done my day's work, and you would know what it was to be tired — and dog tired at that!'

'Yes — I know I'm a lazy beggar.' He said little more during the meal, contenting himself with listening to Vane's cheery talk and quaint tales, of which that good young man always had an abundant supply.

Dinner over, they returned to the library, and drawing two great saddle-bag chairs to the cheery blaze, they lit their pipes and settled down for a quiet evening's chat. Jack stretched himself luxuriously, and threw a glance of keen appreciation round the delightful room. A sudden recollection of his own comfortless 'digs' drew a sigh of discontent from him.

'What a lucky beggar you are, Duke,' he said, as he rammed his pipe full of fragrant tobacco. Then, as he looked sharply at his friend's face, he added: 'Although I must say that you don't look the part at the present moment.'

'I don't feel like it, either,' was the rather grumpily reply.

'Well, what's wrong? Come — out with it; you will feel better when it is "off your chest".'

Duke leaned forward, and poked the fire absent-mindedly.

'I really don't know what is the matter with me,' he said at last, 'but I'll try as well as I can to explain. Of course, I could not speak of it to anyone but yourself.' Vane nodded with perfect understanding, and Duke went on: 'I was at the matinee of *Romeo and Juliet* this afternoon, as I told you at dinner. I happened to be alone, and just turned in to pass the time. I met a girl there, and I haven't been able to get her out of my head for a moment since.'

Vane was silent, and his expression remained non-committal. But inwardly he was smiling, for this was by no means the first time that he had been taken into Duke Percival's confidence in a love affair. He imagined he was hiding his thoughts perfectly until Duke suddenly lifted his eyes — now shining with their strange red glow — and looked him straight in the face.

'I know what you are thinking, Jack,' he said curtly; 'but this is not like the other affairs! This girl is different — she is so innocent. She has only just left her convent school, and knows nothing of the world in which she now finds herself.'

'And she attracted you!' cried his friend, an incredulous note in his voice. 'Good heavens! Duke Percival smitten with the charms of a bread and butter miss!'

'For God's sake, Jack, don't make a jeer of it! It's deadly serious to me.'

And Jack Vane, noting his friend's haggard look and tragic eyes, realised that he must certainly be taking this affair rather badly. Still, that it was anything more than the usual transitory episode he never dreamt for a moment. There had been so many of these in the past! The Spanish dancer at Madrid, over whom Duke had gone quite mad for a brief space; the little Paris model; the singer in London. He naturally supposed this affair would be fleeting also and of no account.

'Well, what are you going to do about it?' he asked.

'Nothing. What can I do?' was the curt answer.

'Nothing? Can you not make her acquaintance?'

'I was formally introduced to her today, as far as that goes. I happened to be at the vice-regal garden party last week, and there I made the acquaintance of a Lady Dempsey — wife of some butcher or publican — trying to push her way into society. You know the sort! She seemed to have found out all about my family, and literally stuck to me for as long as she could. What an hour of boredom I endured by the side of that fat creature! Well, she was at the matinee today, just in front of my seat, and "spotted" me during the second interval. As a matter of fact, I had even forgotten her name until I heard a friend who was with her mention it. But I pretended I was charmed to renew our acquaintance, because I saw she was talking to the mother of the girl who was seated just before me — a little to my left — and to whom I had been drawn in an extraordinary manner from the very moment she entered. After the introduction we were able to talk to each other while her mother went to speak to Lady Dempsey and another dowager a few seats away. She is, as I told you, almost a child; about eighteen in years, but much younger in all her ideas and outlook, and quite undeveloped from an intellectual standpoint. But you know the article which the good nuns turn out from their schools.'

'Well! but if she's that sort, good Lord! what can you do?'

'Nothing, as I told you. I don't mean even to see her again if I can possibly avoid doing so.'

'What is she like? Can you describe her to me?' asked Jack curiously.

'Not very tall — slight figure — pretty hands and feet. She has big grey eyes as absolutely innocent as those of a child, and the most adorable smile! To watch her vivid blush, and then the quick, upward look and smile! I tell you, Jack, that since I left her this afternoon I can see nothing else but her face, and hear nothing but her soft voice and pretty laugh.'

'And do you really mean that you are going to drop her acquaintance at once, and do nothing further?'

'Of course. What else can I do? You know my views on marriage as thoroughly as I do myself. I will never tie myself to any one woman — on that I am resolved. But even if I looked on matrimony — hateful word! — from an ordinary standpoint, a marriage between this girl and myself would be impossible. My aristocratic family would expire! I wish you could just see mother Connor, then you would understand. Therefore marriage is out of the question, and with this girl anything else is unthinkable!'

'Well! if that is so, I would advise you to steer clear of the charmer! What about going abroad for a while — or even paying a visit to Belmont?'

'No, thanks! Besides I cannot conveniently leave town now. Anyway, my path lies far apart from that of the Dempseys and Connors; I shall only have to keep away from viceregal parties and such like, and I'll probably never meet Nora again.'

'Oh! so her name is Nora?'

'Yes. Nora Connor.'

'Well, Duke, I'm sorry for you! You always take these affairs hard. Oh! yes — as the other was about to speak — 'I know that you think this is quite different from the others, and so on, but you know, old man, I've heard that before. And here and now, at the risk of being snubbed, I prophesy that in a week's time you will have forgotten all about Nora Connor, and I shall be listening to a rhapsody from you on the charms of somebody else.'

'You are wrong,' was the sombre reply. 'I will never forget her I can never do so! But at least I will try to avoid seeing her any more, and I don't think it is likely that we shall ever meet again.'

Duke Percival was mistaken. Fate had decreed that he and Nora Connor should meet again, and that, too, before another week had passed.

3

NORA CONNOR AT HOME

It was on a Saturday that Duke Percival and Nora Connor first met. The next morning Nora awoke early, and as she lay in bed, knowing that it was not time to rise, she found herself going over, and over again, all the details of that meeting; remembering vividly every word, every look, of the man who had come so suddenly and so wonderfully into her life.

The Connors lived in Rathgar — in No. 4 Hamilton Terrace. It was a good-sized house of the usual suburban type; there were a few flower beds in front, steps up to the front door, and a fairly large garden at the rear. A commodious house for the family, which consisted only of Mr and Mrs Connor, their son, Harry — at present a student in Trinity — Nora.

The girl had a bedroom at the back, overlooking the garden, and on this fine March morning, when the quiet of Sunday was everywhere, she could hear the chirping of the sparrows in the ivy, and an animated discussion going on in the hen house at the end of the next garden, the hens cackling amongst themselves and the cocks now and then giving forth their clarion crows, which were answered immediately by all the other cocks of the neighbourhood. Nora had always had this room ever since she had been old enough to sleep alone; and when she went away to the convent boarding school it was kept unoccupied until she came back for the holidays. Now that she had left school she had rearranged the furniture and settled the room according to her own taste. In one of the women's papers of that period she had happened to read that 'a colour scheme of pale blue and white is most suitable for a young girl's room' and such a scheme she had adopted. The furniture of her room was very plain and simple, for Mrs Connor had furnished it in the beginning with articles of cheap deal, painted white, which she had considered quite good enough for a child's room, especially as in those days the Connors' grocery establishment was neither so large nor so flourishing as it afterwards became. The original white had degenerated into a dirty yellow with time, so Nora found no difficulty in persuading her mother to allow her to paint it blue. With brush in hand she spent many a happy hour 'doing up' her room. This was the age when the ribbon-bow was chastely tied to various articles of furniture, and especially round the legs of those useless objects which resembled small milking stools. Nora had two of these in her room; the stools she had painted white, and then she tied pale blue ribbon round their legs. Blue bows also were tied to the bed, and used to decorate the dressing table and mirror. On the mantelpiece were photos of her favourite nuns and school companions, and a large one of her brother Harry — whom she almost adores — in his cap and gown. Pictures of various kinds, both religious and secular — most of them being framed 'Christmas Numbers' —were on the walls; and on a bracket over the bed was a lamp burning before a statue of the Virgin and Child

Nora was very pleased with her room, and thought it pretty: indeed, perhaps that word would describe it correctly. She never guessed that such a room would have driven Duke Percival to the verge of insanity. She was thinking of him now as she lay, wide eyed, gazing up at the ceiling, listening for the sounds of the waking household. She had dreamt of him all night. They were confused dreams which she could not now remember clearly; but in all her sleeping visions his face was before her, his red — brown eyes were gazing into her own, and his voice — that soft voice, which was a caress in itself — was in her ears. She could not understand it. Even at confession, the previous evening, she had been thinking of him, until suddenly realising how shocked the nuns would have been at such distraction on her part, she tried to put him out of her mind. But her trying was in vain, and here was she now thinking of him again, when she felt that her thoughts should have been on far different subjects.

'Oh! I must be becoming a very wicked girl!' she thought. Presently she heard movements in the room overhead, where the two servants slept — heavy footfalls which told her that Anne, the cook, was dressing. Then Anne came down the stairs, past Nora's door, to the hall on the ground floor. The front door opened and closed, and Anne was on her way to 7 o'clock Mass, for which the neighbouring bells had just begun to ring.

In a few minutes Mollie, the housemaid, could be heard in the room above. She was young and fleet-footed and was presently flying downstairs to the kitchen to start the morning work.

Nora herself dressed, went to 8 o'clock Mass, and returned to find her father and mother sitting down to the breakfast table. Harry was not at home just then.

The breakfast room was in the basement, as is often the case in such houses. It was a comfortable room, but furnished in ugly Victorian fashion, and a glass door led from it out into the garden.

Mr Connor was a stoutish man in the early fifties. His education was of the slightest — he always said himself that he had learned only the three R's at school — but he had a keen brain for business, and was making money every day. His wife would have liked to spend lavishly, but she was never allowed to go to extremes in this direction, for he — to quote his own words—'held the purse strings'.

Mrs Connor was about the same age as her husband, although wild horses would not have dragged from her an admission of the fact. She looked nearly as old too, for in those days the 'new young' matrons, who dress and behave exactly as do their own daughters, were as yet unknown. Also, women's fashions then were not such as would tend to impart a youthful appearance: quite the contrary, in fact.

On this particular Sunday morning Mrs Connor was attired in a navy blue dress reaching to her feet, and having a high neck. Many rows of braiding were around it, and, of course, she wore the large 'leg of mutton' sleeves which were then so fashionable. Her naturally stout waist was squeezed into the smallest possible compass by the tight corset of the period, and her hair was arranged in a most elaborate fringe and 'bun'.

'Well, Nora,' she said, as her daughter came forward, still in her outdoor coat and skirt, and with her prayer-book in her hand, 'so you have been to early Mass. That's a good girl. I must write and tell Mother Joseph how well you are keeping up to your duties.'

'Hallo, Pigeon!' said her father — 'Pigeon' had been his pet name for her since her babyhood. 'Come here, and give your old dad a kiss.' She had always been his favourite, the very apple of his eye. Left to himself he would have spoilt her — if that were possible with a girl of Nora's character — but his wife would not allow it. She always asserted her belief in firmness, although she showed a lamentable want of it when dealing with the boy Harry, who was her own particular darling.

'So you enjoyed the play yesterday?' asked Mr Connor, as he helped himself to the ham and eggs. 'I hope my little Pigeon won't start gallivantin' around everywhere, or her poor dad won't see much of her.'

'Oh! Daddy, you know that's not likely. But I did enjoy it. It was beautiful.'

A dreamy look came into her grey eyes, and she gazed in front of her for a moment, quite oblivious of the cup of tea which Mrs Connor was holding out to her.

'Come, Nora, wake up!' cried that lady rather testily. 'Surely you want your breakfast.'

The girl took the cup mechanically — the cup in which a pair of red-brown eyes seemed to be laughing up at her as she raised it to her lips. The next moment she almost choked, and set it down hastily as her father's jovial voice said jestingly:'I hope you didn't lose your heart to the handsome young fella your mother was telling me about?'

She could only stare at him, her face scarlet.

'I wish, Joseph, that you would not make such vulgar

jokes,' interposed Mrs Connor. 'You know how I dislike them, and they are never heard in good society.'

'D—good society', is what her husband would have dearly liked to reply, for what was done and what was not done in 'good society' was dinned into his ears morning, noon and night. However, over twenty years of married life had taught him the value of a soft answer.

'Oh! very well — very well, my dear. No offence meant. I am sure Pigeon understands her old Daddy — eh Sweetie?'

The girl nodded her assent, and smiled back at him.

'But I must certainly admit he is a very handsome gentleman,' went on Mrs Connor, 'although, perhaps, the word "distinguished" would describe him better. So aristocratic! Blue blood in every vein!'

'Well, I dunno that I believe much in this blue blood stuff,' said Mr Connor, forgetting his recent rebuff. 'I remember seeing some Lord Tomnoddy or other cutting his finger when standing beside me at a hotel bar, and his blood was as ordinary a red as me own is!'

A crushing retort was on the tip of his wife's tongue, but Nora, seeing it coming, rushed into the breach — a usual task of hers — and said, with a laugh:'Oh! Daddy, what a humbug you are!'

'Humbug is all very well in its own place,' said Mrs Connor coldly, 'but at least I do hope, Joseph, that if Mr Percival should call here any day, and that you happen to be at home — I hope you will remember how to behave.'

'I hope so, too, Mary Ellen,' replied her husband. She detested being called by her baptismal double name, a name for which she had never forgiven her parents. He knew this, and sometimes got a little of his own back by so addressing her. She always signed herself Marie Connor, and was seriously considering whether it would not be well to change the spelling of the surname to *Connyr*. It would be so much more uncommon. Years ago she had prevailed upon her husband to drop the prefix 'O' before his name, ignorant that in so doing she was putting away from herself a mark of an older and better aristocracy than any into which 'the butchers and bakers and candlestick makers', of the present could ever hope to buy their way with money.

'But are you really expecting this young man to pay us a visit?' asked Mr Connor, after a moment's silence.

'Certainly I am. I told him my At-Home day, and he made a note of our address and said he would be charmed to call. Such a perfect gentleman! If you could have seen him helping me into my coat!' And the good lady sighed as she glanced across the table at her husband's honest red face and coarse hands. How noisily he drank his tea and disposed of his ham and eggs! He would never learn proper table manners, she thought.

As for Mr Connor himself, his eyes had strayed to his daughter's sweet face and dwelt there for a moment, as if he was asking himself a question.

Later in the morning, when her parents had gone to Mass, Nora took a book, and as it was fine and warm for March she went into the garden. But she read very little. One subject alone engrossed her thoughts — would he come to Hamilton Terrace? Oh! would he? or had he just promised to do so out of politeness?

The girl knew instinctively, and was able to realise the fact better than her mother, that socially Duke Percival was on an entirely different plane from her own people. The school to which she had been sent was an expensive 'finishing' establishment, where she, the grocer's daughter, had met girls of very different positions and upbringing from her own. Most of them had been fairly kind to her — only a very callous individual would be unkind to Nora — but she still understood the gulf between her and them from a social point of view, and very sensibly made her real friends amongst the girls of her own class daughters of self-made parents, who had been sent there to obtain a veneer of social culture.Therefore, she fully understood that her hero was not of her class. But, after all, when did youth ever allow such matters to become obstacles in the path that leads to Love and Romance? And Nora had not reached the age of eighteen without reading many a thrilling romance in which Love, needless to say, gloriously triumphed over every opposition. Such books were, of course, strictly forbidden in the convent, and for this very reason when chance brought an opportunity of reading one it was all the more eagerly devoured.

Nora had been one of the most avid readers of these stories. No wonder, then, that she at once invested Duke Percival with all the perfections of one of Garvice's finest heroes. Duke was in reality not a divine hero at all — he was a very human sort of person — but nothing could have persuaded Nora into believing this. In her eyes he was all that was chivalrous and ideal — a very knight errant. Women a quarter of a century ago were more romantic, more trustful, and perhaps more foolish in many respects than they are now. And so Nora Connor, as she dreamed away the Sunday morning hours, little thought that her perfect knight would ever fall from his pedestal in her eyes for one moment, or that her love for him would cause her to taste a bitterness worse than death itself.

4

THE SECOND MEETING

On the following Tuesday, about 4 o'clock, Mrs Connor and
Nora were walking down Grafton Street, looking into the
shop windows, and admiring or criticising the fashions of
those days, just as the modern woman admires or criticises
the modes of today. Although Dame Fashion may change,
Eve remains the same through all the ages.

Suddenly Nora felt that somebody's eyes were fixed on
her, and turning her head she encountered the gaze of Duke
Percival.

The meeting was purely accidental: she and her mother
had been standing at a shop window, and Duke Percival had
stopped near the spot to talk to Jack Vane, whom he had just
run across. Duke could not avoid speaking to the two ladies
even had he wished to do so, for already Mrs Connor had
seen him and was holding out her hand with a delighted
smile.

'You will allow me to introduce my friend, Mr Vane?'
said Duke, presently, and then Jack was bowing to Mrs
Connor and glancing curiously at the girl who had been able
to fascinate his fastidious and blase chum. And the more he
gazed at her the more he wondered at Duke's obsession. To
Vane she appeared a very ordinary schoolgirl, pretty,
certainly, but in an immature way. She was so painfully shy,
too *gauche*, he would almost have pronounced her. But
certainly her blushes were delightful, as Duke had said, and
her innocent grey eyes held a very definite charm for a man
— especially a man who had grown world weary, and was
tired of women of a different type

Still, that Duke should fall in love with this little
schoolgirl was beyond his friend's comprehension; and
Vane found himself looking at Percival in amused

bewilderment, and keenly watching his manner towards the young lady. Vane knew of more than one beautiful woman who would have given all she possessed to hear Duke speak to her in those caressing tones and to meet the reddish glow from his strange eyes.

'You will come and have tea?' Duke was asking Mrs Connor. 'Please honour me! My friend and I were just going to have some.'

'Oh! Love! Love! what liars you make of men!' thought Vane to himself, knowing well that tea had not entered Duke's thoughts before this meeting. But he followed the other's lead, and presently the four were discussing tea and cakes at a cosy table in Mitchell's. Vane, having received a very plain hint from Duke, immolated himself on the altar of friendship by gallantly engaging Mrs Connor in conversation, whilst his friend, sitting opposite to Nora, looked into her beautiful eyes with the hungry gaze of one who had longed for the sight of them ever since their last meeting three days ago. Three days! For how many years does that count when one is in love! These two did not talk much — just a few commonplace remarks. Was she tired after the matinee? When was she going again? Just anything to bring to her face that adorable smile and that blush which had so much charm.

And on her part she was content merely to sit and look at him, to listen when he spoke, oblivious alike of her surroundings and of her tea — seven of the cream eclairs so beloved of her schoolgirl soul. And so she would have looked and listened to the end of time, only that practical Mrs Connor at last rose to her feet and announced that they must be going home.

'And now, Mr Percival, when are you coming to see us?' she asked, as they emerged into the crowded street. 'I am At-Home on tomorrow week, the second Wednesday, as I told you. But I suppose' — shaking a fat finger playfully — 'you have quite forgotten all about it!'

'Indeed you wrong me,' was the gallant reply. 'I have kept the date well in my memory and have been looking forward to it with much pleasure.'

Mrs Connor's eyes glowed with pleasure.

'Well now mind, we shall expect you!'

'And yours shall not be vain expectations,' said Duke, as he bowed over her hand.

Jack Vane also received a pressing invitation for the following Wednesday; and while he was making a suitable reply Duke turned for a moment to Nora: 'Will you be glad to see me if I come?' he murmured very softly, as he held her hand. She did not reply in words — but he got his answer all the same.

And then he and Vane were lifting their hats and watching the stout figure of Mrs Connor with the slight one of Nora beside it as they disappeared in the crowd.

Both men were silent for a space as they strolled towards Duke's flat. Then Vane said quietly:'So you have changed your mind, Duke; and I must say you have done so very quickly!'

'Why?'

'Why! Didn't you tell me that you were resolved never to see that girl again?'

'This meeting was not of my seeking, Jack; you must admit that?'

'This meeting? Yes. But what about the meeting at the At-Home next Wednesday? That will be of your own seeking — if you go.'

There was no reply, and the two young men walked a short distance in silence before Vane spoke again. Then he asked in a more serious tone than he had yet used: 'What do you really mean to do about this matter, Duke? Are you going to continue meeting this girl, or will you give her up, as you intended to do at first?'

'Give her up!' cried Duke, with sudden passion, 'No!' and then he added with a sort of quiet bitterness, 'I wish to God I could!'

Vane drew in his breath softly as he glanced at the other's tense, set face; but he said no more, for he knew Duke Percival when these moods were upon him. There was silence between them until the flat in Andover Mansions was reached.

'Come in and have a drink,' said Duke then. Over a whiskey and soda they became confidential, and Duke discussed the matter freely in all its bearings, going over everything with Jack Vane as he could have done with no other man on earth. For these two were perfect friends who had no secrets from each other.

But they could find no way out of the present crux. How could they, when Duke, to all Jack's reasonable appeals, would only say:'I can't! I can't give her up!'

And again:'I tell you, Jack, I never really knew what love meant before! All those other affairs were so different! But this is the real thing — love at first sight!'

'Still, you cannot and will not marry her,' interposed Vane, 'and surely the other way is, as you said yourself, simply unthinkable in the case of a girl like Nora Connor?'

'Absolutely unthinkable. You can take it from me, Jack, that I will never be the one to tarnish her name. Why, it is her perfect innocence and purity that have been such a charm to me. I have seen too many of the other type.'

'In that case — with both marriage and the other kind of relations out of the question — what do you think will be the end of the affair? What do you really intend to do about it?'

'Nothing at present, but just let things drift. I believe in Fate; and you know, Jack, that you are a bit of a fatalist yourself! Don't ask me to exile myself entirely from her just now. Perhaps after a while — if I see that I am really not able to meet her without making a fool of myself — '

'Foolish words, Duke,' broke in Vane, his voice serious almost to sadness. 'If you don't trample on your love for the girl now, you will never do it later on. And constant meetings will only fan the flame. If anything I could say —'

'It's no use, Jack — nothing could change me now. But don't fear for Nora. I'll never cause her a moment's unhappiness; she shall come to no harm through me. That I swear on my honour!'

Vane looked at his friend searchingly. The red-brown eyes were gazing into his, and as he met their straightforward glance Jack gave a sigh of relief. There had been something so appealing in the very youth and innocence of Nora and she had seemed so happy, that he had hated the thought that his own friend should be the one to bring her injury or sorrow. But he knew that to Duke Percival his word was a sacred thing. Never had he known him to fail in keeping a promise. And yet some strange misgiving — a premonition of he knew not what — still seemed to oppress his spirit. He tried to shake it off, but found it very difficult to do so.

He stayed to dinner, and later, but the subject which was nearest to both their hearts was not mentioned again until they were saying goodnight.

Then Duke asked, 'Will you be at the Connors' on Wednesday?'

'Yes, I think I shall,' replied Jack, slowly. But they did not speak again of Nora.

5

A SUBURBAN AT-HOME IN THE NINETIES

Anne, the cook, and Mollie, the housemaid, both detested Mrs Connor's At-Home days — Anne, because she had to make her nicest scones for a number of 'ould wans all dressed up, and not a real lady among the lot av them'; and Mollie, because she had to be dressed for the afternoon earlier than usual, and then remain in the hall to open the door for the visitors. Both of them hated the At-Home function for the further reason that it meant 'herself' paying frequent visits to the kitchen all through the morning hours and wanting a dozen things done at once.

The second Wednesday in March was wet and stormy, and when Mrs Connor came down to breakfast she was very much worried as to whether or not the state of the elements would prevent her At-Home from being the success which on this particular occasion she desired it to be. She did so much want to impress upon Mr Percival the fact that she moved in the 'very best society'; and for that reason had made more than her usual preparations for this special Wednesday. She had ordered rich cakes from town, and worried Anne about the extra light scones she was to make; the drawing-room — hideous beyond words in its crude Victorianism and glaring colours — had been 'turned out'; she had written notes to a few chosen ones amongst her acquaintances, asking them to meet 'My friend, Mr Duke Percival, of Belmont Park, in County Meath, you know.' And her only worry now was lest any undesirable visitors should turn up today, just when they were least wanted. These were a few friends of her earlier days, who sometimes called when she was 'At-Home' — much to Mrs Connor's disgust. But as their husbands were connected with Mr

Connor by business transactions, she had to be civil to them. Some of these had 'progressed' like herself; but some had still remained on the lower rounds of the social ladder.

'I do hope that Mrs Muldoon won't call today,' she said as she poured out the tea.

Her husband was deep in the *Freeman*, reading a speech delivered at a meeting of the United Irish League, and did not lift his head. Nora laughed as she helped herself to toast. 'She is a funny old thing,' she said. 'But I like her — she is so good natured and always has a kind word. Don't you care for her, mamma?'

'Not at my At-Homes,' was Mrs Connor's testy reply. 'And today, you know, I want everything to be extra nice. I'm so afraid the weather will keep some people I like away.'

'I wonder will Aunt Delia come in from Rathfarnham today,' remarked Nora innocently. 'I met her yesterday, and she said that she would try.'

'Nora!' almost screamed her mother, 'what is that you are saying? Is it possible that you actually asked your Aunt Delia to come today — of all times?'

'But, mamma, why not? Surely, I might ask dear Aunt Delia?'

Mrs Connor noticed that her husband's attention was arrested, and that he laid down his paper to listen. So she endeavoured to speak more calmly, knowing what his feelings were about the matter in question.

'My dear Nora,' she replied, guardedly, 'your Aunt Delia is all very well at the right time and in the right place. But at one of my At-Homes, and especially today —'

Her husband interrupted her. It was seldom that Joseph Connor spoke harshly to his wife, especially in Nora's presence; but he was sincerely attached to his only sister, Delia, and could not bear to hear his wife speak of her in such slighting terms. That she was rather old and queer —'a bit of a character' — he knew well, but he knew too — no one better —the sterling worth of the woman. 'What's that you are saying about Delia?' he asked. 'Is she coming today?'

Mrs Connor raised her eyes to heaven as though in pious supplication that such a calamity might be averted. Only that one of her 'lady' friends had lately assured her that it was considered very 'bad form' to cross oneself except at prayer, she would certainly have done so now. As it was, she only murmured fervently, 'Heaven forbid!'

'Heaven forbid, indeed!' exclaimed her husband, 'I'd like to know Mary Ellen, what you mean by that? And I'd also like you to know that my own sister is heartily welcome under this roof whenever she chooses to come —let it on At-Home days or any other kind of days.'

'Oh! very well, Joseph,' replied his wife, sullenly, 'you need not shout. It looks so bad — before the child, too! I am sure I have never objected to poor Delia, altho' she is so odd — even the servants remark it. But I certainly hope she won't take it into her head to come today, when we expect Mr Duke Percival and his friend, Mr Vane. I have asked Lady Dempsey, and several others to meet them. Harry is coming and Julia Murphy will be here, too. And, now, after all my trouble, if Delia should arrive!'

'Well, and what harm if she does? I hope my sister is as honest and as decent a woman as any one of them over-dressed fashion plates that will be here guzzling tea and cakes! And as for them so-called gentlemen, I may as well tell you, Mary Ellen, that I don't care for the likes of them around the place at all. Most likely they're penniless adventurers lookin' after Nora here for her bit of money.'

Nora flushed scarlet, the tears rushing to her eyes. She was very sensitive at all times, and now glanced imploringly at her mother as if asking her to say no more.

'You are quite mistaken, Joseph,' that good lady was saying. 'Mr Percival is a wealthy man, even for his position! An aunt left him a large fortune. He does not even need to practise his profession, but he is ambitious to become famous. The idea of your speaking in that way about such a gentleman — and before Nora, too! Just look at the poor child! No wonder she feels insulted.'

Mr Connor was sorry at once when he saw his daughter's distressed countenance.

'Come here, come here, Pigeon! Don't mind your old dad. Sure your mother has me tormented betimes! Give us a kiss — that's a good girl! But look here' — in a whisper — 'if your Aunt Delia does drop in today, be good to her, won't you?'

'Oh, yes, Daddy, I will! Why, I love her,' she whispered back, pleased as a child and with all her embarrassment forgotten.

Miss Connor was some years older than her brother, being nearly sixty. She lived a few miles beyond Rathfarnham, on the Whitechurch Road; she had a large garden, a field, a cow, a goat, a jennet and poultry of all kinds. Here she worked — milked Daisy the cow, dug and planted her garden, looked after her fowl and ducks, and was happy. A woman from the neighbouring cottages came in to help with the rough work as required; otherwise Miss Connor was alone. Alone, that is, save for her one inseparable companion — a large collie dog, almost human in his intelligence, which rejoiced in the name of Charles Stewart, after C.S. Parnell. Miss Connor had always been an ardent follower of Parnell, and when the split in the Irish Party came, some nine years before the beginning of this story, she was one of those who clung to him most faithfully.

She wore old-fashioned garments and was outspoken almost to the point of rudeness, a characteristic of hers which her sister-in-law both dreaded and detested. There was no foretelling what Miss Delia might say. She had, too, an unpleasant habit of harping on the events of past years, and would sometimes ask Mrs Connor if she remembered certain persons whom they knew, or certain events which took place when the Connors were only beginning life, in the little shop and parlour off Thomas Street.

No wonder Mrs Connor was praying that Aunt Delia might not pay her a visit on this day above all others.

By 4 o'clock that afternoon the drawing-room at Hamilton Terrace presented a gay and animated appearance. A bright fire burned in the well-polished grate, the flames shining pleasantly on the blue curtains and crimson carpet and on the green brocaded furniture — which was kept religiously swathed in holland on ordinary days. The windows were tightly closed, rendering the atmosphere more warm than pleasant. But the ladies of those days, especially those of the 'afternoon tea' type, were greatly afraid of draughts. The day, too, although the weather had improved since morning, was still cold and blustery. Therefore, the hostess was anxiously inquiring — 'You don't feel a draught there, do you, dear Lady Dempsey? I fancy that window lets in a breeze; it does not fit properly.'

'Oh, I am quite comfortable; no draught at all I assure you!' was the gracious response.

Mrs Malone was talking to a Mrs Nolan about the servant question, and two others were discussing pen-painting on velvet, just then a very fashionable occupation. Mrs Connor was ensconced behind the tea table and Nora was helping to pour out the tea, when the door opened noisily and a young man and girl entered.

'Harry, my dear boy! So here you are' exclaimed Mrs Connor. 'And you've brought Julia with you, I'm glad to see.'

Harry Connor at twenty-three was tall and rather inclined to be stout. Built on the same lines as his father, one could easily imagine him resembling the elder man more and more as the years went by. And he had the same honest, straightforward, if rather ordinary, features. By his mother's wishes, but against his own and those of his father, he had been sent to Trinity to study for the medical profession. He had no vocation for the priesthood, and Mrs. Connor considered that it would be nice 'to have a doctor in the family.' Harry himself did not want to go to Trinity, nor did he want to become a doctor. His sole ambition was to be allowed to enter his father's business, and later, perhaps, to be taken into partnership. His father had wished this, too. He desired nothing so much as to see his son succeeding to the good business which as a young man he himself had started. Harry would be spared the early struggles and worries. He would only have to go ahead and make the business better than ever. And Joseph Connor knew that his son possessed all the necessary capabilities, that he had the same instinctive flair for business that had made his father what he was in the commercial world.

But Mrs Connor over-ruled them both in the choice of a career for Harry. He was to be made a professional man — a gentleman. His father's shop must be forgotten by him. And with that end in view the boy was sent to Trinity, where he felt entirely out of his element. Neither did he care for the profession which his mother had mapped out for him. He was now twenty-three, and was not much further advanced in his studies than when he first entered college, and it was his private opinion that he would never see the day on which he would pass his 'Final'.

The girl who had come with him was Julia Murphy, the daughter of a publican in a big way of business. She was an only child, and would come in for a large fortune. A jolly, good-natured girl, good-looking, but rather loud of voice and manner, fond of the slang of the period, and somewhat addicted to boasting about her father's money. She was generally overdressed and wore too much jewellery. But she had a heart of gold and was honestly in love with Harry. Mrs Connor, although wishing that her son had soared much higher in the social sphere than a publican's daughter, condoned his choice in consideration of Julia's fortune. The young couple knew most of the ladies present. Of the sterner sex Harry was, so far, the only representative, and he spoke a few polite commonplaces here and there. But as soon as he and Julia could manage it they slipped away to Nora, where she still remained dutifully near the tea table, her mother having left her in charge while she exchanged the latest scandals with Mrs Malone. Julia and Nora were firm friends, although in many ways they were almost as unlike each other as any two young girls could be. Today Nora, paler than usual, looked like a snowdrop, as she stood by Julia's side.

Both Harry and Julia fancied that Nora was unlike her usual self. If ever a girl possessed 'a heart at leisure from itself, to soothe and sympathise', that girl was Nora Connor. From her earliest years she had been absolutely unselfish — or rather selfless, for she never seemed to think of herself at all. Always ready to listen with sympathy to others, to merge herself in their sorrows or their joys, she was a great favourite with all who knew her. But today she seemed to take little interest in her mother's guests; even her welcome to her brother and his sweetheart was not as spontaneous as usual. True, she was pleased to see them in her pretty, childish way. 'Nora will never grow up,' remarked Julia, slipping an arm through Harry's and then rubbing her face up and down his tweed sleeve, a habit she had had from childhood.

'Well, old girl! glad to see me?' he questioned, in the hearty voice that was so like his father's. She nodded and smiled and lifted her face for Julia's kiss — she always felt such a little thing beside her big sister of the future. But her eyes strayed to the door immediately and both the others noticed that she started slightly, and then that a look of disappointment clouded her face when the door opened to admit a thin 'girl' in the forties with a tiny 'pom' snapping and snarling in her arms.

'My dear Miss Powell, how good of you to come,' cried Mrs Connor, gushingly, 'and darling Fido, too!'

'Who are you watching for, Nora?' asked Julia, bluntly, under cover of the newcomer's entrance, and with her usual disregard of grammar and style?

'Watching for?' The tell-tale crimson raised its flag on her cheek; the snowdrop suddenly became a rose — a rose of love.

'Yes, watching for? Aren't your eyes fixed on the door ever since we came in? Who is it? If it was anyone but yourself, Nora, I'd say it was a young man you were expecting.'

At that moment the door opened again, and Julia Murphy fairly gasped with astonishment.

'My eye and Betty Martin!' she ejaculated, 'Who are those swells? Do you know them, Nora?'

But Nora had not even heard what Julia was saying. She was standing motionless, gazing at the threshold with all her heart in her eyes.

Mollie, in her best bib and tucker, was plainly nervous. While her mistress' oft-repeated injunctions as to how she was to announce the two distinguished guests of the afternoon rather jumbled in her mind, she now flung open the drawing-room door and announced—'Mr Vercival and Mr Pain!'

Inwardly fuming — 'That fool of a girl! I'll give her notice tonight'—but outwardly all smiles, Mrs Connor rose from her seat and went forward with beaming face to greet the young men.

There was a momentary hush amongst the assembled guests, as on the entrance of royalty itself, much to the amusement of the two who were the cause of it; and then Mrs Connor graciously presented them to several of the other guests and to 'my boy, Harry, just run out to see me from Trinity,' and to Miss Murphy. Soon conversation became general again.

Vane and Percival felt that all eyes were upon them, but this fact troubled them not at all; indeed it merely tickled their sense of humour — a sense which was well developed in both. Vane was thinking that some good 'copy' might be got from this handful of very middle-class 'suburbanites'. As for Duke, he had come for one purpose alone and did not mean to waste his time. As soon, therefore, as he could decently get away from Mrs Malone and Lady Dempsey — who claimed him as an old and intimate friend — he went directly to where Nora was standing beside her brother and Julia Murphy. She flushed, and then paled; and quick-witted Julia, observing this and observing also the look in the red-brown eyes bent upon the girl, drew her own conclusions. Duke scarcely looked at Miss Murphy and gave no opportunity for an introduction between her and himself. Sweeping his eyes round the room, now crowded to the point of suffocation, he espied a couch by the folding doors which led into the dining-room. It was empty and was the most secluded spot to be found in the room. There he piloted Nora, and as they sat down he bent his head and tried to look into the sweet grey eyes, which were shyly turned away.

'Look at me, Nora!' he said, softly; and neither of them thought it strange that he should use her Christian name.

She turned and looked at him, and what he read in her eyes robbed him for the moment of speech.

Then he asked, in a whisper: 'Are you glad I came? Did you expect me?'

6

AUNT DELIA

Nora nodded dumbly, and then a smile flashed over her face, and she seemed suddenly to have recovered from her shyness.

'Oh, yes, I am glad — so glad!' she replied. 'I was watching the door for you all the time, and I thought you would never come!'

It was the way child might speak — a child who was gladly greeting some loved friend. Duke recognised this, and inwardly marvelled. Had some of the women he knew spoken in this way he would have understood at once that it was a pose, and treated it as such. But with this girl, whose honest grey eyes told unmistakably of truth and sincerity he knew that the case was different. It was clearly from out of her heart that she spoke. He smiled back at her.

'But I am not late?' he said.

'No, I suppose not. But the time always seems so long when one is waiting for someone, doesn't it?'

'And it seemed long to you?'

'Very long. But now you have come and it's all right.' Then, in sudden dismay. 'Ho! what must you think of me? You have had no tea! Mamma left me in charge of the table. I must go back. Come and have tea, please.'

'No, no! I don't want tea.' Seeing the surprised look in her eyes, he added: 'Vane and I had a cup of tea just before coming out.'

'Oh, why did you! We have such lovely cakes — chocolate eclairs — don't you love them?'

He laughed. 'Do you?'

'Yes, of course. I do love them. We didn't have many rich cakes or sweets at school. I suppose that's why I'm so fond of them. I love chocolates, too, and sometimes Daddy brings me a box of beautiful ones, but Mamma says they are bad for my teeth.'

She laughed and displayed two rows of white teeth, which were so far quite uninjured by those chocolates of Daddy's.

'Mr Connor is not here now?' Duke asked, wondering greatly what sort of man her father might be. Would he be a masculine edition of Mrs Connor? Somehow Percival did not think so. The son was a sturdy, sensible sort of young man, very straightforward looking; and certainly the clear honesty of Nora's eyes was never inherited from her socially scheming mother.

'Daddy very seldom gets home from business before 6 o'clock,' the girl replied, 'and even when he is home early he doesn't come into the drawing-room on one of Mamma's At-Home days.'

'I don't wonder,' thought Duke, with a sudden sympathy for Mr Connor, senior.

'You love your father, Nora?' he said. He did not need to ask the question, for her voice when speaking had told him that much.

'Yes, I love my Daddy. Oh! I wish you knew him; he is such a dear. Not a bit grand, you know, and not a bit like any of these people here.'

She glanced at the overdressed, noisy crowd, who were still engaged in what Mr.Connor had described that morning as 'guzzling tea and cake'.

'These are Mamma's friends,' explained Nora. 'Of course, one has to be polite, but Daddy and I don't care for them.' Then, with a quick change of thought, as she met her brother's rather puzzled look across the room — 'Isn't Harry a darling? and Julia! They are in love' — lowering her voice — 'Isn't it wonderful? And they are going to be married when Harry has passed his "Final".'

'And when will that be?' asked Duke, thinking how much easier it was to visualise young Connor serving behind a counter than standing by a sick bed.

'I don't know,' replied Nora. 'He doesn't get on very

well with his studies. You see, he always wanted to go into the business, but Mamma would not hear of such a thing. She does not like to hear the business mentioned at all. But Daddy tells me all about it' — with a proud little lift of the head. Here was another side to her character, for it was now quite apparent to Duke that in spite of her almost childish ignorance on many matters, she still possessed a fund of sound common sense.

'You are not' — he was going to say ashamed, but changed the sentence to — 'You do not mind talking about the business then?'

'Certainly not. Why should I? Indeed I am very proud of it. Daddy has three big shops now, and he had only one small place when he started for himself. He had been an assistant — just a shop boy — and managed to save a little money. He opened his second shop on the very day that I was born, and it did so well that he always said I was his mascot. Now, he is quite well off, and has a big staff under him. I often wish I were a boy, because then I could go into the business and help poor Dad. I know he feels it very much that Harry is not with him. But when Mamma makes up her mind to a thing Daddy generally has to give in to her wishes.'

'But not always?' asked Duke.

He asked the question idly, more for the sake of hearing her talk than anything else. But it made Nora think of one subject on which her father was adamant and over which he and her mother quarrelled so often — her Aunt Delia.

And at that very moment the drawing-room door opened and the lady of her thoughts stood on the threshold, with a frightened and horrified Mollie in the background. Miss Connor was attired in a rusty black skirt with a bodice to match, and a garment which she called a velvet 'bolero' over this. She also wore a three-quarter length black jacket, which, like her dress, was frayed and rusty, and fitted tightly to her decidedly square figure. On her head was a 'mushroom' hat of yellow straw, with a black ribbon band and strings of the same tied under her chin. She carried a good-sized market basket on her arm, and her hands, brown and muscular — the hands of a worker — were innocent of gloves.

'Here you are, Mary Ellen,' she called, 'these are the eggs and the pair of chickens you wanted. As I see you have company shall I give them to this dressed-up girl of yours?' She threw a glance at the wretched Mollie, and added, 'A good print dress and your sleeves turned up would suit you better, my girl, than all that cap and lace apron nonsense!' She handed Mollie the basket and advanced into the room. 'And while I think of it, Mary Ellen,' she said, 'you haven't paid me for the last eggs and butter I sent you, and I want the money for a pair of boots.'

'Who is she?' whispered Duke, as he surveyed the newcomer, his eyes dancing with amusement.

'Oh! it's Aunt Delia! Mamma will be furious,' said Nora.

Duke Percival, glancing hastily in the direction of his hostess, could well believe that she was furious. Her face was perfectly livid, and she had to moisten her lips before she could speak. That which she had dreaded had happened. Delia, shabbier looking even than usual and in one of her most aggressive moods, had arrived. Poor Mrs Connor's embarrassment was a sight to witness. Hot with shame, she glanced round the room, noticing the supercilious stares, the barely concealed sniggers. Then she rallied her self-possession as well as she could and forced a smile.

'Good afternoon, Delia,' she said. 'What a cold day for you to come! I hope you will not take cold. Did you drive?'

'No, I walked. Kitty — the jennet — had a hard day yesterday carting turf and I wanted to give her a rest. I walked to Terenure and then got the tram here.'

'Walked from Whitechurch on such a day! Oh! Aunt Delia how tired and cold you must be!'

There was no mistaking the real affection in Nora's fresh young voice. She went quickly to Miss Connor's side and kissed her warmly. 'Come over to the fire here and have tea — I'll have some fresh tea made for you,' she said.

'Ah! Nora, my girl. So here you are, and not too grand to speak to your poor old Auntie. I'll be glad of the tea, and that's a fact. My old bones are getting stiff. And indeed I suppose you feel that way yourself sometimes, Mary Ellen? There's not much between us as far as years go.'

Nora, somewhat to Mrs Connor's relief, piloted her aunt to the fire, and seated her comfortably in an armchair. But what was Mrs Connor's horror when she saw Mr Percival hovering beside the old lady. At all costs he must not meet Aunt Delia.

'Oh! Mr Percival,' she said, leaning over the back of her chair to beckon him. 'I want to introduce you to Miss Powell, she is so anxious to meet you.'

'In a moment, Mrs Connor,' was the polite reply. 'I am just making the acquaintance of Miss Connor.'

And a minute after Mrs Connor could hear the clear voice of her daughter — 'the little idiot' — as she gaily made the introduction: 'Aunt Delia, this is Mr Percival — my aunt, Miss Connor.'

'O'Connor, child — O'Connor,' was the testy interruption. 'How many times have I not told you not to leave out the Irish Ó — the grandest title I possess.'

Duke bowed lower over the wrinkled, brown hand which she offered him. His heart warmed to Miss O'Connor — we will give her the proper title in future — for he recognised at once the sterling truthfulness and honesty of the woman. Hating shams himself, he respected her for hating them also.

Had she been a duchess in his mother's drawing-room at Belmont, Duke Percival could not have shown her more deference. While Nora poured out fresh tea for her, he carried her cup and saucer and arranged them on a little table beside her chair, and then, returning laden with plates of various kinds of cake, he asked her to say which was her favourite.'Just an honest bit of bread and butter, or one of Anne's scones,' she told him. 'None of that fancy rubbish for me.'

Untying her hat strings as she spoke, she tossed the hat

on the back of her chair, and then drawing up her skirt planted her two feet in their queer boots on the fender.

'And who may you be, young man?' she asked, as Duke brought her a second cup of tea.

Mrs Connor had now given up all hope of winning him to her own side of the room, and contented herself with murmuring to all and sundry — 'My husband's sister — very eccentric! In fact, not quite — you understand. Such a trial for us all.'

'I told you, Aunt Delia,' interrupted Nora, in answer to Miss O'Connor's question, 'this is Mr Percival.'

'One of the Percivals of Belmont?' asked her aunt quickly.

Duke smiled.

'Yes — those are my people.'

'Well, what are you doing amongst this crowd,' demanded the lady. 'I know of your family and a little of your history, altho' you may be surprised to hear me say so. And I should think that there is no one of your class here, except, perhaps, that young man over there,' and she nodded her head in the direction of Vane. That gentleman was now seated beside Miss Powell, whose simpering 'girlishness' was boring him almost to death, although, for politeness' sake, he outwardly exhibited a polite interest in all her remarks. Duke understood the situation, and, happening just then to catch Jack's eye, grinned cheerfully at the victim.

'Yes, that's Jack Vane, my greatest friend, he said to Miss O'Connor. 'And as to why I am here — well, I was introduced to Mrs Connor last week, and she very kindly asked me to call.'

Miss O'Connor merely said 'Humph' — but when she said it, it meant a good deal.

'Get me some fresh boiling water, there's a good girl,' she said to Nora. 'This tea is a bit too strong for my taste.'

Then as Nora went away she looked keenly at Duke.

'Mr Percival,' she said, 'I just wanted to tell you that if the attraction that is bringing you here is my niece — well, you had better keep away in future! There could be no match between you, as you know, and I am not going to see the girl suffer a heartache for your sake. Don't think for a minute that I don't consider her good enough for you! I can tell you, Mr Percival, that my niece, Nora O'Connor, is good enough for the best man that ever had a pair of brogues on his two feet. But a marriage between the two of you would be madness, as you and I both know. You may think it strange,' she added, more quietly, 'that I should speak to you like this on our first meeting, but I know every turn and twist of Nora, for I love the child. And I saw her eyes when they looked at you — aye, and yours, Mr Percival, when you looked at her.'

Duke was silent, while he stared in frank amazement at the speaker. After all, what could he reply to her words? She looked at him, too, and when she spoke again, her voice held a note of entreaty.

'Keep away from her, Mr Percival,' she said, 'keep away.'

'But Miss O'Connor — '

'Hush! here's Nora; keep your tongue quiet,' was the sharp retort, as the girl came towards them.

'Now, Aunt Delia, here is your hot water,'she said.

Meanwhile Mrs Connor was beginning to think that her sister-in-law's visit was really going to pass off better than she had expected. She appeared to be comfortably settled by the fire drinking her tea, and even if she did say some dreadful things to Mr Percival, Mrs Connor herself could explain to him afterwards that Miss O'Connor was really not quite — you know! He would surely understand.

However, her satisfaction was short-lived, for Aunt Delia, having finished taking tea, was now thoroughly warmed and refreshed, and turned towards the visitors with the intention of joining in the general conversation.

During a lull in the talk the loud voice of Lady Dempsey could be heard distinctly.

'Your tea is really delightful,' she was saying to her hostess, with just a shade of patronage in her tones, for, after all, she had a title — a year old — and never forgot it — 'and as for the cakes! Mitchell's of course?'

'Well, for my part, I must say that I prefer a good home-baked griddle cake any day, to all those Frenchified concoctions,' remarked Miss O'Connor. 'I remember, Mary Ellen, a very nice soda cake you used to bake in the old pot oven that you had hanging over the fire in the parlour behind the shop off Thomas Street. And oh! blessed hour! do you recollect the day that the child came in for a farthing's worth of sugar stick, and you were so mad at having to leave your baking for such a customer that you boxed her ears? Glory be! I can see you yet, your sleeves turned up — and fine arms you had in them days, Mary Ellen, for baking and scrubbing, and your hands all flour! 'Tis little did either of us think then that you'd ever be sitting in a swell drawing-room eating cream cakes!'

There was a petrified silence for a moment amongst the guests, and then poor Mrs Connor, speechless and wretched, saw with thankfulness that her visitors were collecting their furs and gloves and preparing to depart. 'The best thing they could do,' she thought. She was ruined in 'society' after this; and as she mechanically acknowledged their adieux, she felt that for herself life was no longer worth living.

Duke Percival was one of the last to leave. He had stayed for a final word with Nora, even under the keen eyes of Miss O'Connor. As he held his hostess's hand, she tried to make some excuses for her sister-in-law — she was so eccentric, no one minded what she said, and so on.

But Duke laughed.

'I assure you, Mrs Connor,' he replied, 'that I thoroughly enjoyed my little chat with Miss O'Connor. I found her a most unusual and interesting lady, indeed.'

His voice had a note of sincerity which compelled her to believe what he said, but although believing she could not understand. She only smiled vaguely as she turned to shake hands with Jack Vane.

'The Lord be praised,' said that young man, as he found

himself on the Rathgar Road; 'and Heaven forgive you, Duke, for letting me in for such an afternoon. But never again!'

Duke laughed pleasantly.

'I have spent a most delightful afternoon,' he said.

Meanwhile when the last callers had departed, Mrs Connor turned to her sister-in-law who was still comfortably seated by the fire, and if looks could kill, Delia O'Connor had expired then and there.

'Well! Delia,' she said, in tones of such concentrated fury that Nora's face blanched. 'Well, I suppose now that you have ruined and disgraced me for ever in the eyes of society — made me the laughing-stock of Dublin — I suppose you are satisfied, and will take your departure?'

'You may suppose what you like, Mary Ellen,' replied Miss O'Connor, as she took a pinch of snuff. 'All I can say is that you are even a bigger fool than I thought you were. And don't be shouting like that and scaring Nora here. If those are lady-like manners, I prefer me own. As to taking me departure, I intend waiting till me brother comes home from the city, as I want a talk with him. But don't let me detain you, ma'am. Nora and I will be very happy here.'

7

THE MARRIAGE OATH

Just outside a small village which lies between Dublin and Blessington there is a little Catholic church, and there on the morning of 12 August 1899, Duke Percival and Nora Connor were made man and wife. Jack Vane was the only friend who was present at the ceremony, and indeed, but for him it would have been scarcely possible to get a priest to marry them at all. Jack knew the priest in charge of the church intimately, for as boys they had been neighbours and companions. By what scheme of deceit he had tricked his reverend friend into performing the ceremony heaven only knows. It is certain, at all events, that Nora was represented as an orphan alone in the world, and that her age was given as twenty-one, although she was really only eighteen years and a half, and looked even younger than that. However, they were married, on a perfect summer's morning, with Vane and the deaf old clerk as witnesses.

The few months following that breezy March day, when we saw Nora at her mother's At-Home, had been a period of sheer bliss for the girl. Duke had thrown all his sensible resolutions overboard, and, deliberately refusing to face the question of what the ultimate issue might be, started a violent siege of the girl's heart. Vane had done all that a mortal could do — without severing their friendship — to persuade his friend to 'see reason', as he phrased it. Senior to Duke in years, and wise through the remembered experiences of a love tragedy in his own past life, he had endeavoured, both for Duke's own sake and for that of the girl, to persuade his friend to 'give it all up', had urged him more than once in fact to leave the country, in the hope that a change of scene might cause him to forget 'this little schoolgirl', as he called Nora on these occasions. There were times when Jack felt vexed with Nora for having crossed Duke's path, but on calmer consideration of the matter he had in common justice to admit that all the wooing was on the side of his friend. The lovers had gone everywhere together during those glorious days of spring and summer, with Mrs Connor, of course, as chaperon, for there were chaperons in the nineties. But Nora's mother knew when to efface herself at times; she could be comfortable and contented in a chair near the bandstand at Bray or Kingstown, while the young couple went for a stroll along the quiet parts of the promenade or pier. But most delightful to Nora was the band in the Sorrento Gardens at Dalkey on Saturday nights. There she and Duke could wander away at will in the scented dusk of the summer night; it was there one night, with the soft lap of the Irish Sea in the distance, and the strains of 'For Ever and for Ever' wafted to them from the band, that Duke first spoke to her of his love, and laid his first kiss upon her pure lips.

With innocent delight she spoke of telling her parents, but when he begged her to keep their love a secret for a little while, she consented — readily indeed, for his slightest wish was law to her, but still not without a pang of regret. She had never had a secret from them before, and said so to Duke in a tone that conveyed more than a suspicion of disappointment; but he reassured her in a lover's way, and with his arms about her she was content. That had been early in July, and Mrs Connor, knowing nothing of their secret engagement, waited daily for the formal proposal which she felt certain was coming. Nightly she talked about it to her husband, rather to his annoyance. He had met Percival and had taken a fancy to him, whilst Duke, on his part, really liked Nora's father, with his plain, honest face and outspoken ways. But still Joseph Connor was by no means satisfied with the condition of affairs between Duke and his daughter. Only for his wife he would have asked the young man straight out as to what his intentions were; but Mrs

Connor would not hear of such an idea. She was afraid it might alter in some serious way the trend of things which seemed to her mind then to be quite satisfactory; and the very thought of losing a Percival of Belmont as her future son-in-law was too terrible for words.

So things had drifted on, Duke always the guest of honour at Hamilton Terrace as far as his hostess was concerned, but regarded with some uneasiness by Mr Connor and with open suspicion by Harry and Julia, who both openly declared that 'the bloomin' swell did not mean marriage.

The affair was never mentioned at all in Nora's presence. When Duke was spoken of it was as an ordinary friend, except, indeed, that Mrs Connor would allow herself to smile and look wise now and then. The girl herself was of such a sensitive nature that none of them would risk saying a word that might agitate her. That she loved him they knew, for she could not hide the fact from them. She had tried indeed to do so; but the flush on her cheeks, the love-light in her eyes, when he drew near her — these she was powerless to veil from their sharp glances. And thus, suspecting that her heart had gone out to Duke, they worried greatly about her — all of the family, that is except her mother.

This attitude of complacency on Mrs Connor's part greatly annoyed her son.

'He'll never put a ring on her finger, mother, I'm telling you that,' he said one evening, when he was at Rathgar. 'Don't I know his sort? He to marry a grocer's daughter!'

'If I thought he was trifling with her — just carrying on a flirtation to please himself — I'd soon kick him out of the house,' said Mr Connor.

'Aye, and I'd help you to do it, Dad,' said his son.

'Oh, how foolish you both are,' cried Mrs Connor. 'It is perfectly plain to be seen that Mr Percival is paying attention to Nora with a view to matrimony. Doesn't he come here and meet her openly in the presence of her family, like the honourable gentleman that he is? What more do you want? He is just waiting until he is sure that the dear child's heart is won — she is so young. But he will speak soon — of that I am sure.'

'Well, maybe you're right,' said her husband. 'I must say I rather like the chap meself, he seems decent enough.'

'Decent enough, yes — in his own way,' interrupted Harry, 'but he won't marry out of his own class. Some swells do it, but he's not that sort. I know fellows in college who know his people, and they have told me all about them. They are as proud as Lucifer, especially his mother, and he thinks an awful lot of her, although she is as cold as ice. His brother, Everard, is not married yet, and if he were to die this Duke chap would inherit the estates. I tell you, Dad, he will never marry Nora; he's only philandering around the girl — and it's high time it was put a stop to.'

'Well, I'll tell you what I'll do,' announced Mr Connor slowly, 'and mind you, Mary Ellen, this is me last word on the matter, for me mind is made up. I'll give the bucko till the second week in August — that's a month — and if he hasn't come to the point by then I'll send Nora off somewhere out of Dublin. When she's gone I'll have a word with Mr Duke Percival, and give him his marching orders. The girl could go to those school friends of hers in Wicklow — you know whom I mean, Mary Ellen —the ones she promised so often to visit. Anyway she will be best away until the affair blows over and she forgets all about it.'

'You needn't worry over that, Joseph,' said Mrs. Connor serenely, 'everything will be satisfactorily arranged before that time.'

'Well, I hope so, I'm sure,' replied her husband, adding, 'but what I've said stands, and don't you forget it Mary Ellen.'

The first week in August had come and gone, and the second, and still Mrs Connor was eagerly waiting for Duke's proposal. It did not come; and Nora was informed that her father thought she was looking pale, and so for her health's sake she was to write and arrange to pay her long-promised visit to the Byrnes, who lived a few miles beyond the town of Wicklow.

Both her parents were secretly surprised at her readiness to fall in with their wishes, but little did they dream what was the reason for it.

Duke had at last persuaded Nora to consent to a secret marriage. It had not been easy; all the girl's ideals and instincts had been against it; she hated deceiving her parents — the very thought of keeping her marriage concealed from her father was bitterness unspeakable. Then, too, came the religious question. Duke had told her frankly that he was an Agnostic, but her look of horror, her instinctive repulsion from him for the moment, had made him regret being so open. She could not comprehend such a state of mind, and never had he been so near losing her. He sensed it immediately, and tried by every means in his power to retrieve his mistake.

'Of course, sweetheart,' he said, 'I will never interfere with you. You can go your own way and attend to your religious duties as often as you like. You will be perfectly free in all these matters. And if — if there should be children, you can train them in your own faith.' He won her over after a little. Perhaps she thought — as women will think to the end of time — that her love and her prayers would save his soul. Was it not then plainly her duty to marry him? And so she consented. She was to start for Wicklow. It was such a short journey that she was luckily allowed to travel alone, and she was to leave the train at a nearer station where Duke would be waiting for her, and from there they were to drive to the little church where they would be married. Everything fell out as they had planned. She stepped out of the train at a little wayside station, and there Duke — a radiant impetuous Duke — met her with a dog cart and high-stepping mare. A drive of some miles brought them to the church, where Jack Vane, who had been waiting at the gate, came forward and helped her to the ground. Very grave and quiet Jack seemed to be, but very kind and gentle too. He kissed her on the forehead after they had all signed the register in the homely little sacristy, and wished her every happiness. His tone was very grave, almost solemn, she thought, but she knew his good wishes were sincere.

He said goodbye to them both at the church gate and went back to Dublin, whilst they drove away towards Roundwood,where, in a most delightful cottage, the honeymoon was to be spent.

Luck had certainly been with them. Kitty Byrne was one of Nora's greatest friends, and would do anything in the world for her. Nora had written and told her that she was visiting another friend for a fortnight first: that it was a great secret; but that she would know all about it very soon. And would Kitty help her by posting in Wicklow any letters Nora sent her, and also send on at once any letter that came from Dublin for her? Kitty Byrne, although naturally curious about the secret, promised faithfully to do this; and also to make things smooth with her own people. So that was settled satisfactorily. Two weeks were to be spent among the Wicklow hills with him who was now her husband; and then she was to go to the Byrnes in Wicklow. How long her marriage was to be kept secret she did not know. Duke had asked her to trust him, and she had given her promise to do so. Besides, she was now his wife and so bound to love and obey him. She sat beside Duke now, silent from sheer happiness, as the dog cart bowled along the dusty country road, and the hot August sun shone above them.

The cottage Duke had taken for their honeymoon was up a laneway off the main road. It contained just four rooms; there was a queer old garden at the back, and some flower beds were in front of the door. A high and thick yew hedge hid it from the road. It was thatched, and roses were climbing all over the old porch and nodding in at the open casements. Duke had heard of it from a friend, and was delighted to be able to rent it. He had taken it by the month, as he really did not know himself what his plans were to be.

When the dog cart stopped at the little gate of Woodside Cottage, Pierre Lamont was standing there awaiting his master. There was a stable at the end of the garden, and the Frenchman led the horse there. When he returned Duke and

Nora were still standing at the garden gate looking across at the beautiful Wicklow mountains.

'Pierre,' called his master.

'Monsieur.'

'This lady, Pierre, is the mistress of this cottage. You will obey her orders in everything; and treat her always with the same respect and honour, the same devotion, that you give to myself.'

Pierre bowed low.

'Monsieur has spoken,' he said. 'Madame shall be obeyed.'

As he turned away, Nora looked after him in slight surprise. She had met Pierre before. Twice she had gone to tea with her mother in Duke's flat, and on several occasions the servant had come to Rathgar with messages or notes from Percival. But there was something in the Frenchman's manner now, perfectly trained though he was, which puzzled her. He had looked at her. She hardly knew how to describe his look — but it was one she did not like.

'I think Pierre is sorry that you are married,' she said with a little laugh.

Duke's face darkened.

'It does not matter what he thinks,' he said shortly. 'Come along and see the cottage.'

And a dear abode it was. Queer, low-ceilinged rooms, with chintz-covered chairs and strange old prints on the walls; a bedroom with furniture draped with dimity muslin, and here, too, the roses were nodding in at the diamond-shaped windows. Such a cottage! One would think it had been built specially for a summer honeymoon of love and roses. So Nora was thinking that evening when after one of Pierre's delightful dinners they came out to the porch to watch the moonlight on the hills.

An hour went by as they sat hand in hand — 'the world forgetting, by the world forgot.'

Then Duke said, 'I want to speak to Pierre, Sweetheart; wait there till I return.'

Pierre was in the little kitchen, just preparing to retire for the night. Everything was in spotless order; the kitchen boy, of course, had been left in town, but the Frenchman's deft hands had all as it should be.

'Pierre,' said his master abruptly, 'I want to speak to you about the lady who is here with me.'

Pierre spread out his hands, and raised eyebrows and shoulders, plainly meaning: 'It is of no consequence to me, Monsieur; do not trouble to explain.'

'You are mistaken,' said his master quietly. He spoke in French for fear that Nora might hear a word in the silence of the house. Although she had a 'learned French' at school, and was supposed by her parents to know it well he was fairly certain that the Parisian French which he and Pierre so fluently used would not be understood by her. At his words the Frenchman stood looking at him in silence.

'You are mistaken,' repeated Duke. 'The lady with me is Madame Percival, my dear and honoured wife. We were married this morning. You and Mr Vane — who came to the church — are the only two who know of it. I was not going to tell you — I did not mean to do so — but—but, I could not bear that you should think her to be other than she is.'

Pierre's face was transformed — he was plainly delighted.

'Oh! Monsieur!' he cried, 'I wish you all the happiness your heart could desire! Ah! but I am glad. I was so sorry for Madame today, I thought — but Monsieur will forgive?'

'It was but natural, Pierre,' replied Duke, rather sadly, 'and now will you give me your solemn promise not to speak of this marriage to any one, under any circumstances — until I give you permission?'

'Oh! Monsieur, of course, I swear it solemnly.'

Duke returned to the porch, and a few minutes later Pierre Lamont came through the open door and stood beside them.

'Yes, Pierre?' said Duke.

'If I might be permitted,' said the Frenchman in his best English, 'if Madame would allow, that I wish her great happiness, and what you call such good luck!'

Nora laughed gaily.

'Oh! thank you, Pierre,' she said, delighted to see the change in the man; 'you are very kind.'

Pierre bowed low.

'Monsieur permits?' he asked, and lifted Nora's slim hand to his lips.

The girl felt instinctively the respect in his manner, which had been missing before, but she was far from comprehending the reason.

When they were left alone Duke said to her: 'Nora darling — my little wife — I am going to ask you to show your love and trust by doing something for me. Will you do it?'

'Oh! Duke! My beloved. Need you ask? What is it?'

He hesitated, and she asked again, 'What is it? Don't you know that I will do anything in the world for you?'

'I want you to take a solemn oath — to swear by that which you hold most sacred — not to reveal to anyone, under any circumstances whatever, that you are my wife, until I give permission to do so.'

There was silence for a moment, and the girl at his side shivered as though she were suddenly cold.

'Well, sweetheart — will you do this for me?'

'Why? Oh! beloved, tell me why I must do this thing? Why must we keep it so secret?'

'Only for a little while, sweetheart! It's on account of my mother. I've never told you about her. She is very proud, and some people think her hard, but I was always her favourite son, although Everard is the heir. She would not think that you were a suitable wife for me. We know she is wrong, of course, but she is ill now, and the doctors say that any shock might kill her. So I want to wait awhile, and if she gets better I will tell her all about you in my own way and my own time, and she will love you when she sees you. But I am so afraid she might hear it some other way. I love her, Nora, although she is not a woman of a lovable type; most people think her very cold and severe. So will you promise me, sweetheart?'

And so Nora Percival took the oath her husband wished, repeating the words slowly after him as he pronounced them: 'I solemnly swear by all I hold most sacred never to reveal that I am married to Duke Percival. I will never tell the fact to anyone, and never acknowledge my marriage under any circumstances whatever, until my husband gives me his permission. So help me God.'

'And now, sweetheart, what do you hold most sacred?' he asked.

'Why, this, of course,' she replied, and drew forth a little silver crucifix from the bosom of her white frock.

'Then kiss the crucifix to seal your oath,' he said.

She bent and touched the emblem of her faith with her innocent lips. And surely the very angels above must have wept if they knew what that oath was to cost her.

8

THE END OF THE HONEYMOON

Nora Percival stood in the porch of Woodside Cottage the next morning, and thought what a very beautiful world it was that she lived in. And if this old world of ours would not be beautiful amidst the peaceful loveliness of the Wicklow hills at nine on a summer morning, to one who is young and in love — why, it could never be beautiful in one's eyes at any time.

Nora went down the garden path to the gate, and resting her arms on the top of it she drew in great breaths of the pure air, while her gaze wandered along the little lane to the road beyond. There was not a soul in sight, and the only sounds were the voices of the birds, the most persistent of which was the monotonous call of the wood-pigeons from the wood at the end of the cottage garden. Presently, from an adjacent field, came the whirr of a reaping machine, the crack of a whip, the sound of a man's voice shouting to his horses. Then a country cart passed the end of the lane, and soon came the shrill voices of children from a cottage down the road. The morning was very hot, but Nora looked delightfully cool in her white linen gown. As she had been going, or pretending to go, on a lengthy visit she had brought quite a large number of dresses with her. Her father, too, had given her a generous cheque to spend in 'faldlals, and such rubbish!' Probably he thought, poor man, that it would help to soothe her wounded heart.

She is very, very happy on this, the first day of her married life; happy with a kind of wonder and awe, that such a man as Duke should ever have stooped to a girl like herself, and glorified her life with his love. For so she thought in her humility, he had done, and if anyone had suggested to her that far from being the perfect knight, the Sir Galahad she thought him to be, Duke was only human — and very human at that — she would have scoffed at the idea.

The only bar to her perfect happiness was the necessity of keeping the marriage a secret, especially from her own people. She knew that her mother was bitterly disappointed because — as she thought — Duke had not spoken. Nora felt this acutely, particularly when she remembered that lately Mrs Connor had been particularly kind and affectionate to her; as also her father and brother, each in his own way. She could only console herself with the thought that all this subterfuge and secrecy would not last for long. The truth would be confessed as soon as Lady Percival was either completely recovered, or gone where no worldly troubles would worry her. Then would Nora be able to announce to the world the glorious news that she was Mrs Duke Percival.

'Mrs Duke Percival!' She repeated the name softly to herself, and lifting her left hand to her lips, proudly kissed the broad band of the wedding ring which Duke had placed there yesterday in the little church that nestled at the foot of the hill.

'But I may not say anything until he allows me. Not a word.'

The remembrance of the solemn oath which she had taken the previous night cast a shadow on her happiness, and for a moment a cloud rested on her fair young face.

But almost immediately the cloud lifted as if by magic. Only the everyday magic of love; just his voice calling down the garden path: 'Sweetheart! Where are you, sweetheart? Breakfast is ready.'

She turned to meet him with shining eyes and radiant face, as he came towards her, and with his arm around her they went back to the house, into the quaint little parlour, where breakfast was laid on the round table, which Pierre had drawn up to the open casements. The summer breeze gently stirred the white muslin curtains and brought with it the perfume of the nodding roses and honeysuckle, the sweetbriar hedge and the new-mown hay — the hundred and one scents of the countryside on such a morn as this.

When Nora sat down she found a couple of beautiful crimson roses with the dew still on their leaves, beside her plate.

She looked at her husband.

'No,' he said, replying to her unspoken question. 'You needn't thank me. I was not wandering in the garden early enough to find those.'

'Then who — ?' she was beginning to ask. But at that moment Pierre entered with one of the breakfast dishes, and at once she guessed that he had gathered them for her.

'Pierre,' she cried. 'Did you gather those roses for me? Oh, I know you did. How nice of you to think of me!'

Pierre bowed low.

'Madame will deign to accept?' he asked, and as Nora nodded smilingly, he said, 'Ah! the roses! They are like Madame as she is this morning, all glowing with love and life. And are they not the flowers of love?'

Duke laughed.

'When you know Pierre better,' he said, 'you will understand that he is a very sentimental person indeed.'

'There is one thing certain,' he added, when the Frenchman had left the room, 'you have completely won his heart. He will be your slave for evermore now.'

'And I like him very much,' replied Nora. 'When we first came here yesterday I thought that he seemed angry, and not pleased to see me. But I see now that I was mistaken.'

'Quite mistaken,' said Duke, 'Give me another cup of tea, sweetheart. I could drink a dozen just to watch your little hands pouring it out for me.'

And so the days went by — dear, dear days of love and happiness to which both of them would afterwards look back with a kind of despairing wonder that such bliss had indeed once been theirs.

The weather was ideal, and they spent most of their time

out of doors. The tiny wood at the end of the garden, where the wood-pigeons cooed their perpetual love stories was a favourite spot with them. There in the shade of the trees they would sit through the summer hours, Duke sometimes reading aloud, with his arm round his wife's waist, and her head on his shoulder, whilst at other times they would just talk and talk — as lovers will.

Now and then they went for drives in the high dog cart, with Molly Bawn, the well-bred mare from Belmont stables between the shafts. At first Nora was a little bit afraid of the high-stepping animal, but after a while she and Molly Bawn became fast friends, and the mare would whinny when she heard Nora's voice, and nuzzle at her hand for sugar.

They never went far afield in their drives, as even here there was no knowing that they might not meet some one of those whom they most wished to avoid. So far their solitude had been unbroken. Pierre went every day to the village and called at the post office for letters according to arrangement. He professed to know but a word or two of English, and this staved off any curious questions from the postmistress.

Nora received a letter from her mother, in reply to one she had herself written and enclosed to Kitty Byrne, asking the latter to post it in Wicklow. She very much disliked this deception, but realised that it was necessary in the circumstances. She had only written a few lines, saying that she had arrived safely, and was having an enjoyable time. All quite true, of course, but — Nora hated the writing of it.

Mrs Connor's reply was long and full of trivial details and small happenings; also of advice as to how Nora was to behave. It advised her as to what she had best wear on such and such an occasion; and also warned her not to say up too late at night. There was no reference to Duke, until the very end of the letter, and then came the sentence which Duke laughed over: *'We have seen nothing of Mr Percival since you left. I do not like to believe it, but I am very, very much afraid I was mistaken in him — and I thought he was such a gentleman.'*

Duke laughed, as we have said, but he checked the laughter quickly, when he saw that Nora's eyes were wet.

'Why, sweetheart — what is it?' he asked.

'Nothing — at least, not much. Only — oh! beloved — I hate to think of Mamma being deceived like that. I feel so mean about it all.'

Don't sweetheart. Don't worry. It is only for a little while. Think how she herself will laugh over the whole affair by and by.'

So he rallied her, and loyally she tried to respond. But sometimes she experienced a strange fear — a dread of the future, which assailed her, in spite of all her present happiness and her love for and absolute trust in Duke. And he had been so good to her! He have been lover, husband and brother, all in one, she thought sometimes. She was such a child; she had married knowing so little of the facts of life; and Duke had, during the honeymoon, acted towards her as a very perfect knight.

One evening they wandered to the end of the wood, and on to a lonely bit of mountain road where the bracken and yellow gorse grew thick and high. In one spot it was trampled and the ground charred, and here they came upon a gipsy encampment.

There were two caravans, with the usual high steps and tiny windows bedecked with curtains. The horses were nibbling at the short grass, and dogs and children were playing around everywhere. A big cooking pot was boiling cheerily over a fire of sticks, and a withered old crone was watching it. A few men were sprawling on the ground, and two very handsome, bold-faced girls, wearing gaudy handkerchiefs on their heads and big gold earrings, gazed fixedly at Nora.

As she and Duke drew near, the old woman noticed them. 'Let me tell your fortune, pretty lady,' she cried. 'Let the gipsy read your hand.'

At this moment a young woman, with a baby in her arms, came down the steps of one of the caravans.

'Oh! what a lovely baby,' cried Nora; and the woman,

hearing what she said, smiled, and came towards them.

It was certainly a very pretty and interesting baby, healthy and brown, as only an outdoor child can be, and with firm, tanned little limbs. It was a boy baby about nine months old. After staring solemnly for a moment at Nora, with its great black eyes, it laughed and crowed, and stretched out a friendly hand. She held up a finger, and it was at once caught and held tightly in the baby fist.

'Oh, Duke!' Nora cried, 'Isn't it a darling! Give me something to give it.'

He thrust his hand in his pocket and drew out the first coin he felt. It was sovereign, and Nora took it from him with a laugh of delight.

'My baby must have it,' she cried, and held out the glittering coin to the child.

The mother expressed her thanks effusively, and when she had skilfully abstracted the coin from the baby's hand — 'for fear he would swally it, lady' — and given him a crust instead, she looked keenly at Nora.

'Give me your hand, lady,' she said, 'and I'll tell your fortune.'

With a laugh the girl held out her hand, and the gipsy looked intently at the soft little palm.

'A wife,' she said slowly, 'a wife today; but afterwards a wife, and yet no wife. Trouble — trouble with sorrow, and a weary journey, with a sore heart and bleeding feet.'

With a face that was pale and frightened, Nora drew back her hand and shivered.

'Here, my good woman,' said Duke, angrily, 'if you can spin no better yarn than that stuff, you had better say no more.'

But the woman did not seem to hear him. She took Nora's hand again in her own brown one, and gazed at it, a strange look in her dark eyes.

'When your time of sorrow comes, lady,' she said then, very gently, 'keep a brave heart. And in your hour of your sorest need, may you find comfort and solace, and a friend to help you, as you have helped Rachael Lee today.'

Nora stood looking at her, pale and troubled, unable to read the meaning of the gipsy's words.

'Come on, sweetheart,' said Duke, 'don't listen to any more nonsense. It's time we were getting back to the cottage.'

The gipsy turned to him swiftly, her eyes searching his face.

'Well, what do you see?' he asked scoffingly. 'Have you a tale of woe for me, too?'

'Give me your hand,' she said quietly. And, impelled in some strange way almost against his will to do so, Duke held out his hand. A hand that was typical of the man's character, the hand of a dandy, well kept and beautifully manicured; but a hand too that was as strong and flexible as though it were made of living steel. The gipsy studied it in silence for a moment, and then she spoke.

'A hurried journey before another day has passed; a sick bed.'

In spite of himself, Duke felt uneasy. His mother was constantly in his thoughts just then, even in the midst of his great happiness.

'Afterwards — a long journey across the ocean, and then war — red war.'

Duke laughed in relief. After all the woman was only a charlatan. War, indeed! What next?

'Do not laugh,' said the gipsy. 'You will think of my words one night, when you lie on a battlefield many and many a mile away. And for the sake of her who wears your ring today — the ring that will leave her finger before twenty-four hours are gone — may luck be with you.'

She turned and went across the grass to the caravan, the black-eyed baby looking back over her shoulder at Nora, and continuing to laugh and crow with evident delight.

After dinner that evening, as they sat in the porch and watched the last bit of daylight disappear behind the hills, Nora spoke of the gipsy.

'What could she have meant?' she questioned. 'I do not

understand what she meant was to happen to me. But, you, oh! beloved — what can she mean by war and battlefields?'

'Oh! just the usual catch-penny tales,' cried Duke contemptuously. 'But you needn't worry about me, sweetheart. I can jolly well look after myself any day — and after my sweetheart wife as well.'

He gathered her tenderly into his arms, and within their loving shelter she forgot every trouble and worry, and remembered only that she was living in a beautiful world, and that Duke loved her.

The next day Jack Vane came for lunch. Duke had written and asked him to come.

'We have been ten days here now,' he wrote, *'and it has passed like one day of perfect happiness. Come along, old pal, and see for yourself how marriage agrees with one who had sworn never to bear its yoke.'*

And in truth Duke's marriage had been one of the biggest surprises of Vane's life. Again and again had he heard the other declaim against marriage, and all that appertained to it; affirming that the idea of a man and woman living together for the whole of their lives, until separated by death, was ridiculous and absurd. Of divorce also Duke had often expressed his dislike, protesting that having to pay money and go through the law courts to obtain a separation was unfair and unjust. He held that a man and woman once they wished it, should be at perfect liberty to separate and look elsewhere for fresh partners.

'A change of husband and wife is as essential as a change of scenery,' he had often said to Vane. 'If one gets tired so often of the same streets and towns, and hills and valleys, how much more tired one would get of the same face sitting opposite one at table for every day of the year.' And, therefore, when Duke had told him that he intended to make Nora Connor his wife, Vane had been positively dumbfounded.

'I knew all you would say,' Percival had said quietly, 'and I understand how astonished you must be. But I love this girl, Jack, as I never thought to love any woman. I love her with the reverence and love which a man gives to a pure woman. Therefore, as our laws and customs stand at the present day, nothing remains for me but to make her my wife. Could you, by any flight of imagination, think of anything else in connection with Nora?'

'No,' replied Vane, 'I could not.' After a moment he asked, 'Will you marry her in the Catholic Church?'

'Yes — she wishes it. The religious ceremony means nothing to me, of course, but it means everything to her. I shall be satisfied with any ceremony that makes her my wife in the eyes of the world, even although the marriage must be kept secret at first, on account of my mother.'

And so after a long talk all arrangements had been made, and Vane had promised to do all he could to smooth matters with Father Black.

He had done so, and now on this blazing day, at the end of August, he was going to see the result of that which he had — partly against his will — helped to bring about.

Duke met him at the wayside station and drove him to Woodside Cottage, where Nora stood at the gate watching for them. Such a happy radiant Nora! Vane, as he looked from her face to that of Duke, felt a sudden pain, a tightening of the heart strings which made him wince, as if at the re-opening of an old wound. Even so had he himself once looked at a dear, dead love of years ago.

Duke, whose instinct was as keen as that of a woman, understood at once what was passing through the other's mind, and with an affectionate gesture took him by the arm and led him to Nora.

Her welcome was very real, and she played the hostess with such childlike dignity, that Vane was both amused and touched.

There was no need to ask if they were happy; he could read the answer in their every glance. Yet Jack, with a sort of sad cynicism which always clung to him, found himself wondering how long it would last.

Looking to all the circumstances of the case as he knew

them, he saw the strongest reasons to fear that the marriage would ultimately turn out a failure. Lady Percival would be furious, and as she ruled Sir Roger (her husband), and also her son, they would probably turn the cold shoulder to Duke. From a monetary point of view, it would not matter to him, as he was possessed of ample private means of his own, besides the income from his profession; but Duke, even though he disliked living at Belmont, still had an inherited love for and pride in the old place. It was 'home' to him always, and he would feel it strange, indeed, if its portals were closed to him. Besides, he had a very real regard for his father, and for his brother, Everard. His mother he loved; and a break with her would cut him to the heart. She was in poor health at present, and Vane knew that Duke was anxious about her, and that it was on this account that he had taken such infinite precautions to keep his marriage a secret. He probably meant to go and see her himself, and break it to her in his own way, when she got better; but Vane could not imagine Lady Percival — whom he knew well — ever forgiving such an act on the part of her favourite son. He tried to picture Lady Percival and Mrs Connor in friendly conversation, but his brain recoiled from the effort. Even Nora herself did not seem to fit into the scheme of things at Belmont. Certainly she was not vulgar, like her mother, on the contrary, she was unaffectedly well-mannered and naturally refined; but yet between her way of life and that of the mistress of Belmont there was a wide gulf.

Love, of course, had blinded Percival to all this, but when the inevitable awakening came — how would he feel it?

Lunch passed off very pleasantly, Pierre having been careful to remember Jack's favourite dishes. The latter found himself alone with the Frenchman for a few minutes during the afternoon.

'Well, Pierre,' he asked, 'how do you like Madame?'

'Ah! Monsieur Vane — an angel. A saint sent to us by *le*

bon Dieu. Such happiness for Monsieur!'

'Mr Duke told me that he had let you into the secret,' said Vane.

'But yes! At first I thought — but no matter! And I could not bear to think it and she so young and innocent and a good Catholic. I might have known better — imbecile that I am.'

Later, sitting at tea in the garden, watching Nora's pretty hands at the teacups, and Duke's loving glance resting on her bent head, Vane thought, not for the first time, what an enviable lot was that of his friend.

'What a lucky beggar you are, Duke,' he said, just as he had said once before on that night when Duke first told him about Nora. And now he added meaningly: 'And this time you look the part to perfection.'

Duke glanced at him, and then remembered to what he was referring. He flung back his handsome head and laughed joyously.'Yes, and this time I feel it, too!' he replied.

Nora looked up from pouring out the tea to ask what was the joke, and Duke had started to tell her, when they were interrupted by Pierre coming towards them with a salver in his hand.

'A telegram for Monsieur.'

Duke, the laughter frozen on his lips, put out his hand. When he had read it, both Vane and Nora knew that it was bad news.

'Beloved — what is it?' she asked in a frightened whisper, laying a hand on his arm.

His own tightly closed over it as he said, in a strange expressionless voice —'My mother is ill — dying, they fear. I must go to Belmont immediately.'

9

PARTED

There was a train to Dublin at eight o'clock that evening from the little station beyond the village. Duke decided to go by this; but he did not know whether he could get a train to take him that night from Dublin to Belmont. He was afraid he would have to wait in Dublin till next morning. and was anxious and worried. Vane would return to town with him and it was settled that Nora should remain at Woodside Cottage until Duke could find out how matters stood at Belmont. Should he not be able to return to her in a few days she was to go on to Wicklow and pay her promised visit to Kitty Byrne. But for a time she would be all right at the cottage, as Pierre would be left in charge of her.

'And you can trust him absolutely, sweetheart,' said Duke, as they stood together in the old-fashioned bedroom which Pierre had just left, carrying his master's suitcase. Nora was feeling dreadfully lonely and miserable. For Duke's sake she was trying to look brave and cheerful; but this blow had fallen so unexpectedly that she felt completely crushed.

'I will write to you as soon as I reach Belmont, and every day as long as I may have to remain. Of course, sweetheart, your letters will come under cover to Pierre — you won't mind, darling?' for he had seen the quick flush which sprang to her face when she heard his words.

'No — I'll try not to mind. But oh! beloved, I had so looked forward to watching for my letters —the first addressed to Mrs Duke Percival.'

'But, sweetheart, your letters could not be addressed in that name. Not yet anyway. You haven't forgotten your promise? And now there is something else, darling. I want you to let me take off your wedding ring, and you will keep it safely until I put it on again. Keep it with your marriage certificate — here it is. I want you to have this in your own possession. But always remember not to speak of our marriage to any living person until I give you leave. I know I can trust you, can I not, sweetheart?'

'Oh! beloved, yes. I will keep my oath at any cost.'

'That is my own little girl! And now let me take off the ring, for no one else shall take it off, or put it on your finger except your husband. Not even yourself.'

But she drew back with a cry of pain.

'The gipsy,' she exclaimed. 'Oh, Duke, don't you remember?'

And Duke suddenly seemed to hear again the voice of Rachael Lee saying — 'The ring that will come off your finger before twenty-four hours are gone.'

And it was just twenty-four hours since she had spoken. He stood rigid for a moment, while Nora buried her face against his coat and cried piteously.

'Oh, Duke, my beloved! let me keep my ring.'

'It is impossible, sweetheart,' he said, his voice harsh from the effort he made not to break down. 'It is out of the question. How could our marriage be kept secret if you openly wore your wedding ring? Wear it in that little silk affair that you have round your neck.'

'That is the bag in which I keep my medals,' she said.

'Well, put your wedding ring with them, and the certificate too, it will fold up small enough. And now be brave, sweetheart,' he added, as he quietly slipped off the plain gold band and handed it to her. 'Think of the day — and it may be very soon — when I will come back to you to put the ring on your finger, never to have it taken off any more! And then, if my mother lives, I'll take you down to see her.'

Nora nodded and tried to smile.

'That's better,' cried Duke, and stood to watch her as with deft fingers she sewed the ring inside the little silk bag and slipped in the certificate, replacing carefully the religious medals and emblems.

'And now I must be off,' he said. 'It would never do if I

missed this train.'

'Say goodbye to me here, beloved,' she pleaded; 'don't ask me to go downstairs.'

'But, sweetheart, it's not like a real parting; why, to look at you one would think that I was going away for a year! Come down and wave goodbye from the gate.'

'No, I'll wave from the window here. Kiss me goodbye now, beloved.'

He folded her in his arms and their lips met in one long breathless kiss.

This kiss of Nora's was a revelation to Duke; for even loving him as she did, she was, as a rule, shy and slightly reserved, so that she seldom allowed her feelings to carry her away. But now it was as if she would pour forth all the love of her heart in this one kiss. He had to remove her arms gently as they clung round his neck, and when he saw her face he felt a tightening of the throat and a mist before his eyes.

'Sweetheart,' he cried, 'how I wish I had not to go, or that I could take you with me. But don't feel it like that; it's only for a little while.'

'God grant it, beloved,' she said. 'Go now, and God be with you.'

Strangely moved, Duke left her and ran down the few stairs to the tiny hall, where Vane stood calling out to him to hurry or they would be late for the train.

'Where is Nora?' he asked.

'She is staying upstairs,' replied Duke. 'She's rather upset, and said that she would wave to us from the window and not come down again.'

They went out to the waiting dog cart, where Pierre was standing at the mare's head; he was coming with them in order to drive the cart back again.

As Duke sprang to his seat and seized the reins, he looked up at the window where Nora stood, framed, as it were, between the diamond lattice panes with their fluttering curtains and the nodding pink roses. She was wearing one of her favourite white frocks, and although her face was

pale, she was smiling bravely as she waved her hand to him
— the pretty slim hand he loved so much.

And thus, in all her young beauty — like some lovely
picture — Duke was to see her on the pages of his memory
for many and many a day.

He hardly spoke during the drive to the station, and
Vane, understanding, left him to his thoughts. He turned,
however, for a last word with Pierre as the train was coming
into the station.

'Now, you quite understand all my instructions,' he
said, 'about the letters and everything. And if Madame goes
to Wicklow, you will see she journeys in comfort. I leave
her as a sacred charge to you, Pierre, until I return, or until
she goes back to her people. Guard her as the very apple of
your eye, or you will answer to me!'

Pierre bowed, and then straightening himself, looked his
master squarely in the face and said, simply, 'Monsieur need
not have said that. Madame will be safe with me'.

When he returned to the cottage all was very silent; no
lights showed in the evening dusk, and no waiting figure
stood by the gate or in the porch. Pierre took Molly Bawn
round to the stable, and having unyoked and attended to her
wants, he entered the house by the back door, which led
from the garden.

Silence everywhere. At first it seemed to him that he
could hear nothing at all. Then a sound broke upon his
listening ears — the low, gentle sobbing of one who has
sobbed, and sobbed, and is tired. Few sounds are so pitiful
as the steady monotonous sobbing of a woman who thinks
she is alone and has abandoned herself to her grief.

For a little while Pierre hesitated. She was such a child
that he had almost decided to go and comfort her, as he
would have done had she been a child in very deed. But his
intuition told him that Nora would not like it — she would
wish to keep her dignity.

'La pauvre petite,' he murmured under his breath, and
crept softly back to the kitchen. An instant later he re-entered
by the back door, banging it after him, and making quite a

noise by moving chairs about and clattering fire irons.

Nora sat up suddenly. She had been lying, face downwards, on the old chintz-covered sofa, and now, remembering her flushed and tear-stained face, she tip-toed from the room and up the stairs.

In the kitchen Pierre smiled to himself. 'It is well she goes to repair the ravages of grief.'

As far as ducking her face in a basin of cold water and brushing her hair would repair such ravages, Nora did her best.

Then she went downstairs calling out, 'Are you back, Pierre? I thought I heard you.'

'But yes, Madame. I have this moment returned. Madame will have some coffee before she retires?'

'No, nothing, thank you, Pierre. I am not hungry.'

'Ah! but that will not do. Monsieur has given to me the care of Madame. If, when he returns, Madame is pale, he will be angry — so angry, with Pierre Lamont! Madame will have some hot milk and just two little aspirins, and then she will go to sleep and dream of Monsieur.'

Nora smiled wistfully.

'How did my husband look?' she enquired. It was so delightful to say — 'my husband'. She always felt two inches taller when she spoke the words. And now she was enquiring about his appearance, as if she had not seen him for a year at least.

But Pierre understood.

'Monsieur was in the best of health and looking forward to the reunion with Madame.'

'He seemed sad at the thought of leaving me?' she asked.

'Ravaged with sorrow! A man of a broken heart for the moment, but consoled at the thought of his speedy return to Madam.'

And thus he cheered her with all the wit and charm of his nation, and Nora, in spite of all her strange forebodings and vague presentiments, fell asleep on this her first night of loneliness, with a smile on her lips. The next day she received a letter from Mrs Connor in which that lady said that she and Mr Connor were going over to the Isle of Man for a fortnight. She had not been feeling very well and thought the change would do her good. She was so glad that Nora was enjoying herself, and she was to stay a while longer in Wicklow if Mrs Byrne would be so kind as to have her. They were crossing to the Isle of Man immediately, and she would write again to Nora when they arrived.

Somehow this letter made the girl feel doubly lonely. In a few days the sea would divide her from her dear Daddy, and she had a great longing just now for a sight of his honest face and kind, homely talk.

She went into the sunny kitchen, and perching herself on the end of the table watched Pierre as he deftly rolled some pastry.

'What are you making, Pierre?' she asked.

'An apple tart for the lunch of Madame. Does not Madame like apple tart?'

'Yes, I love it,' replied Nora. Marriage had not made her less schoolgirl in her mode of speech. Then she laughed: 'It's so funny to see you making pastry,' she said. 'Anne, our cook at home, is such a fat old thing. She makes nice tarts, too, but they are not as light as the ones you make.'

'That is not to be expected,' said Pierre, with patronising dignity.

'Can you make eclairs — chocolate ones?' asked Nora.

'But, of a certainty. Does Madame care for them?'

'Care for them? I love them! Please make me some to-day, Pierre; they might cheer me up! And I feel so lonely now that my husband'— again the proud inflection in the girlish tones — 'is away. And I have just heard that Mamma and my dear Daddy are going for a trip to the Isle of Man.'

'But that is nothing — the journey of an hour or so!'

'But I do feel lonely. Pierre, you know my husband a very long time don't you?'

'For five years, Madame.'

'Well, that's a long time, and you understand him. Why! I have only known him five months. And yet he loves me.

Don't you think he loves me very much, Pierre?'

Pierre paused, rolling pin in hand, as he exclaimed dramatically: 'But yes — Monsieur adores Madame! Never have I seen him so much in earnest before.'

Nora sat up straight.

'Before? But, Pierre, he has never loved before he met me. Never. He told me so.'

Pierre, inwardly raging at his own blundering stupidity, hastened to retrieve his tactless error.

'Oh! Madame. Of course, I meant that never had I seen him so earnest about anything, or so anxious about anything, as he is about the comfort of Madame.'

Nora, of course was satisfied, but later Pierre tore his hair in the solitude of his own room, while he cried: 'Imbecile that thou art, Pierre Lamont! And that innocent angel!'

Nora stayed for a while longer chatting to Pierre, and then said she would go for a walk before lunch.

'That is good,' said the Frenchman. 'Madame will then have the appetite for the tart of apple! And for the tea of Madame I will make the eclairs of France!'

But still that first day seemed endless to Nora, and try as she might she could not banish a feeling of sorrow and depression which weighed heavily upon her spirits. The next day she had a letter from Duke. How hungrily she watched for Pierre returning from the post office, and the moment she caught sight of him how eagerly she ran down the lane and literally snatched the letter from his hand. She fled into the parlour and tore off the covering envelope, which was addressed to Pierre. She had hoped to see the magic words — *Mrs Duke Percival* — on the inner envelope. But the words she had looked for were not there; one word only, the word *Sweetheart* was to be read on it.

'Sweetheart'. She could almost hear his voice again calling her. That dear voice, which she had not heard now for so many years as it seemed to her.

Duke wrote that his mother was very ill and weak. The doctor had ordered her to keep perfectly quiet and to avoid the least worry of any sort. She wished him to stay, and he would have to remain for at least a couple of weeks, or until there was a change of some kind in her condition. Nora had better decide to go to Wicklow at once; there was a letter enclosed for Pierre to make all arrangements. He would write to her there and let her know what was best to be done.

And the rest of the letter was just for her own ears alone. Over and over she read it. With passion it told her how much he missed her, how he longed for her, and longed for the day that would unite them, never to be parted again — the day when he would replace the ring on her finger and proclaim proudly to the world that she was his wife. He loved — he loved her! And her spirit was with him by night and day.

She kissed the words and blotted them with her tears. 'My beloved — oh! my beloved,' she whispered.

The next day she went to Wicklow, and was met at the station by Kitty Byrne, a good-natured girl of nineteen. Kitty was full of curiosity as to Nora's secret friends, but, needless to say, she never guessed the truth. The nearest she got to it was that there had been an 'attraction' where Nora was staying, and that 'he' did not have the approval of Mrs Connor.

Nora let her think what she liked. She would have dearly liked to take Kitty into her confidence, but as that was not possible she kept her friend's curiosity laughingly at bay, only promising that 'some day she would know all about it'.

Her father and mother both wrote from the Isle of Man, where they were evidently enjoying themselves in their own way, for they had decided to stay on for a third week, which would bring them into the middle of September. Duke wrote daily, as he had promised, but had little news to tell her. His mother kept about the same, and he was still obliged to remain at Belmont. Then one evening, just a few days before the expected return of Mr and Mrs Connor, Nora, coming in with Kitty from a walk, was surprised to be met in the hall by Mrs Byrne. Kitty's mother was crying, and coming to Nora she put her arms about her.

'Nora, my dear,' she began.

'Oh! mother, what is it?' cried Kitty, for Nora could not speak.

'Nora, your brother has come; there is bad news; try to be brave — '

For the moment Nora had an impulse to cry aloud — 'Is it Duke?' But then, remembering that Harry would not be coming if it was about her husband, another fear gripped her heart.

'Daddy,' she whispered. 'Oh! Mrs Byrne — my dear Daddy.'

Then she saw her brother's burly figure standing behind Mrs Byrne, and the next moment she was alone with him, standing in the wide hallway with his strong arms around her, while he was whispering brokenly, 'My dear little girlie! Oh! Nora darling — there's just the two of us now! Just the two of us left.'

Mr and Mrs Connor had been drowned in a boating accident off the Isle of Man coast. They had gone boating with several other tourists, and from some cause the boat overturned, and the Connors and one other had been caught under the boat, and when taken to land were dead.

To Nora the next few days seemed like some terrible nightmare, from which she must surely awaken soon. She could not realise that she would never again in this world see her father's face or hear his kindly voice. She had loved him very dearly; he had been everything to her from the days of her childhood. When sitting on his knee she could coax from him anything she wanted. She tried to realise that he was gone—really gone out of her life — but realise it she could not; every moment she found herself listening for his footsteps and watching for him to come in at the door.

Her mother she grieved for too, but she had never had the same great love for mother as for her dear Daddy. To Nora's sorrow for her mother was also added something more terrible than any grief—the feeling of remorse. Remorse, deep and bitter, for having deceived Mrs Connor about her marriage with Duke. Oh! if only she could have mother back again just for a few moments to assure her that she had not been mistaken in Duke — that he was still the gentleman she had always thought him.

'Oh! Mamma,' wailed the girl wife, 'it grieves me so deeply that I could not tell you. But it is all right as far as Duke's honour is concerned, and oh! I hope you know now that it is.'

But was everything all right? Sometimes it seemed to her that no blessing could follow this secret marriage. How soon after it trouble had come upon her! The death of her parents made a great change in Nora's life. Harry left Trinity, and gave up his studies for the medical profession. He took his father's place in the business, and proved himself a worthy son of honest Joseph Connor.

He was very troubled about Nora. She never seemed to have got over their loss; she grew very pale and was strangely quiet. So Harry, thinking things over in his mind, spoke to Julia Murphy and her family, and it was agreed in the circumstances, both for his own sake and for that of Nora, he and Julia should be quietly married. His house wanted a capable mistress, and both he and Nora needed someone cheery and sensible beside them to help them over their trouble. So not very long after the tragedy Julia Murphy was married to Harry Connor, and took up her residence as mistress of No. 8 Hamilton Terrace.

And on the whole Nora was glad. It had been very dismal when only she and Harry were together, sitting often in silence, always conscious of two empty chairs beside them. Julia, in her own way, brought much life and cheerfulness with her. She was sincerely fond of Nora and was very good to her.

Duke wrote constantly and his letters were the greatest comfort she had in her sorrow. But Lady Percival was not getting any better, and Duke could not leave her side, even for a day. Nora must only be patient and trust that he would come to her the very first moment that he possibly could.

10

THE MISTRESS OF BELMONT

In her great 'four-poster' mahogany bed, propped up with pillows, Lady Percival was slowly, but surely, breathing her life away. Very rapid and difficult, too, was the breathing at times, very blue and pinched were the thin features. But the indomitable spirit, the iron will, of the woman had not weakened. From her death bed in the great bed chamber she ruled Belmont now, as she had ruled it when she was able to make her daily round of house and grounds. And ruled it thoroughly and well — from the master, Sir Roger, down to the newest kitchen maid and gardener's boy.

Belmont was a big building of grey stone. The original house had been built in Cromwell's time, and it had been added to at later dates by various Percivals. Lady Dempsey had been mistaken when she informed Mrs Connor that the family were Anglo-Normans. The first Percival to land in Ireland had done so in the army of Oliver Cromwell, and so well did he please the latter that he was rewarded with the grant of the castle and lands belonging to a certain Desmond O'Toole, who was a noted 'papist and rebel'. Of the old castle nothing remained but the keep, now a roofless ruin and in great request by the rooks of the neighbourhood. Visitors to Belmont passed this relic of another race as they walked up the avenue to the house. None of the servants or people around would go near it at night, as it was said to be haunted by the spirit of Eithne O'Toole, the young wife of that Desmond whom Cromwell had dispossessed and robbed of his heritage.

The house stood on a gentle rise, overlooking much of the surrounding country; a magnificent avenue lined with grand old trees led up to the nail-studded oaken door at the top of the stone terrace; the surrounding grounds were noted for miles around, as were also the beautiful gardens. Lady Percival had always been an ardent lover of gardening, and she and old Angus McNeill, the dour but clever Scotch gardener, had not only made the gardens of Belmont a picture of rare beauty, but had turned them into a good paying concern. Not only her fruit and vegetables, but her flowers, too, found a ready market in the Dublin shops. She also closely superintended the dairy and poultry; it was a common belief in Belmont that a hen could not lay an egg without her ladyship being cognisant of the fact.

She had been a splendid mistress for Belmont, and a valuable wife and helpmate to Sir Roger, who was of a rather easygoing disposition; and as the estate had been heavily mortgaged by an extravagant Percival of two generations back, retrenchment and economy had been very necessary. Lady Percival had seen to it that expenses were reduced, and not only that, but, as we have seen, she had made Belmont more than pay its way. So that now, when she knew her days were literally numbered, she had the satisfaction of also knowing that the last payment on the mortgage was made, and that Belmont was free of debt.

Previous to her marriage with Sir Roger Percival she had been Margaret Eaton, the daughter of a small landowner in the south. One of many children, she had brought her husband only a small dowry. But he had not cared; he was genuinely fond of her, and her thrift had been worth a fortune to him since their marriage.

She was fifty-five — not so very old in years; but she had always had a weak heart, and now she knew that the end was very near — a matter of days, or at most of a few weeks.

So the doctor had told her when she demanded to know the truth — demanded it in her old imperious way. To her family he added that all excitement and worry — the least trouble of any kind — must be carefully kept from her. Worry might prove fatal any moment. A cold woman, very reserved by nature, she had one weakness—if weakness it could be called — and that was an intense love for her younger son, Duke. She had had but the two boys — there was no daughter — and Duke had always been her especial favourite. Everard, the heir, was like his father, fond of country life, a keen follower of the hounds, interested in prize cattle, and in his horses and dogs. A complete contrast to Duke with his artistic temperament and love of travel and study. The one sorrow of Lady Percival's life was that Duke had not been born the heir instead of Everard. The difference in their ages was only a little over a year, and yet she often thought what a difference it meant to their future. The lady of Belmont had grown to love every stone and corner of the grey old mansion, every tree on the estate, every flower in the garden. Sir Roger had never possessed her heart; she had never pretended that her marriage had been for her any other but one of convenience, although she always yielded him what she called 'wifely duty', and a sort of cold friendship. But the love she denied to her husband and her elder son she lavished on Duke, and — in a different manner — on Belmont, her home now for the past thirty-five years.

On this fine October morning she was sitting up in bed gazing out of the window, from which she could see the sweep of the long avenue, and in the distance the ivy covered tower of the ruined keep. In spite of her illness she did not look her five and fifty years. Her hair was still abundant, with scarcely a tinge of grey showing on it, and her eyes were as bright as in the days of her youth.

She touched a bell on the small bedside table, and immediately her maid entered. This was Dorcas Prim, an intensely respectable female, very plain, very evangelical, and — a standing joke at Belmont — as prim as her name.

'You rang, m'lady?'

'Yes, Prim. Kindly request Mr Duke to come up now, and ask him to bring the morning papers with him.'

A few minutes later Duke entered, in his hands the *Irish Times* and *Daily Express* of the day.

He stooped and kissed his mother with real affection, as he asked her how she felt. Although far from loving her with the great love which she had for him, he still sincerely loved her. Next to his love for Nora, which was now the great love of his life, came his love for his mother.

Her face changed and softened as she kissed him back, putting up a frail hand to touch his cheek for a moment.

'And what is the news this morning?'she asked presently.

Of late it had been Duke's daily task to read the papers to her, for she was a keen politician and took a great interest in the affairs of the day. Just then trouble was looming very near for the British Empire, to which Lady Percival was intensely loyal. The news in the papers that day was very definite; but Duke, not wishing to excite her in any way, made as light of it as he possibly could.

'There's going to be a little trouble in South Africa, after all, mother,' he said. 'I see those Boer fellows are taking the field.'

He read her further details while she listened keenly. The Anglo-Boer War was at its commencement. On 11 October 1899, the Boer Government informed their people that the time specified for England's reply to their ultimatum had elapsed, and that, therefore, hostilities must begin. That same evening part of the Boer Army had crossed the frontier into Natal, and the war had begun.

That was what Duke read to his mother on that autumn morning, when the leaves were falling in the avenue of Belmont, and the cawing of the rooks could be heard from the old keep.

'But, of course, it will be all over in no time, mother,' he said, as he put down the paper. 'The Boers will have surrendered by Christmas, if not sooner.'

His mother was silent for a moment.

'Very likely,' she said then; 'it is not probable that they will be able to stand against our army for very long. But, still, one never knows. I believe they are a very obstinate people.'

'Still, they are only farmers — not really drilled or trained. Why, mother, the whole affair will fizzle out in a month's time.'

'It may be so. But, Duke, if it should not — if this war should last any considerable time, and if the empire should call for men — promise me that you will be one of the first to volunteer for active service to fight for your queen and country.'

Duke rose to his feet and strolled across to the window, where he stood gazing with unseeing eyes at the trees in the avenue and the glimpses of blue sky above.

Although he had been brought up in the ranks of extreme unionists, he was yet absolutely indifferent to politics. He looked upon them from the point of view of the student and the philosopher, believing that all political parties were, more or less, corrupt — simply out for their own selfish ends. But he was sufficiently imbued with the convictions of his class to regard Irish Nationalists with deep dislike. The so-called Irish Nationalism of that day was very poor stuff, and not likely to appeal to Duke Percival. Real Irish ideals were unknown to him: Irish Ireland was a closed book, as far as he was concerned. Certainly he had read about the Gaels of old, but he looked upon all that had been written about their achievements as being more or less in the nature of a fairy tale. As for the men of later periods who had suffered and died for their country — they were 'rebels'.

But, all the same, Duke was no ardent loyalist either, and he did not see at all why he should now be called upon to help England in her battle against this little South African Republic, that had so pluckily thrown down the gauntlet to her. England would win without his help, and, of course, he would be glad to see her winning — one must be loyal to the empire. But still he didn't like the idea of going off to South Africa. And besides there was Nora, the sweetheart wife, whose loving letter of that very morning rested next to his heart — Nora, light-hearted and gay as she walked beside him during those dear days of their honeymoon, and Nora, framed amongst the roses, as she waved goodbye to him on that parting day, and tried to smile through her tears.

How could he go to South Africa and leave her behind? The thing was impossible. Let them fight their own battles

— Boer and Briton. He didn't care if a hundred empires called him. Nora reigned supreme over them all in his heart.

But, on the other hand, there was his mother. What if her heart was set on his going? He knew so well her rigid, unbending loyalty; her bitter antagonism towards those in Ireland who had ideas different from hers regarding the claims of the empire. And the doctor had been so insistent that she should not be worried or thwarted in any way.

Duke Percival cursed the tangle in which he found himself, as he stood at the window, staring blankly down the avenue and seeing nothing.

'Why do you wish this, mother?' he asked then, without turning his head.

His mother's voice answered him in a tone of genuine surprise: 'Why should I not wish it, Duke? It has been the custom, as you know, for all the younger sons of Belmont to fight for the crown, when the crown needs their help. The heir stays at home, as is only right.'

This custom had been followed at Belmont ever since Cromwell have given its fair lands to the first Percival. Duke knew it, of course, but strange to say, he had quite forgotten all about this tradition of his family, until reminded by his mother.

Had it not been for Nora he would not have cared much one way or another. A war — even a small affair, such as he thought this would prove — might be interesting; he and Jack Vane might have some jolly experiences together. But his marriage put another aspect on the whole business. Of course if his mother knew of the step which he had taken she might not press the point. But she must not know of it.

'Mother,' he said hesitatingly, 'there might be circumstances — something might happen to prevent me from going — to keep me here —'

'What could prevent you from doing your duty — your plain duty as a Percival?' she interrupted, her voice shaking with anger. 'There is nothing to keep you here! You are not married — you have no ties of any sort. And, as for me — I will not be long alive, as you know.'

He was on his knees by the bedside before she finished speaking; patting her hands, telling her it was all right, not to worry — he would go, of course he would go.

All the time two remembrances were tormenting his mind — both fighting for mastery. One was the memory of he doctor's words; 'the least excitement or annoyance may prove fatal.' The other was the memory of his girl-wife waiting and watching for his return.

But his mother was looking at him, her eyes searching his face, her countenance livid, with the dreaded blue tinge on her lips; her breath coming in gasps.

'Then, you promise, Duke? I have your word — the word of a Percival — that, at the very first call for men which the empire sends out you will volunteer? Give me your promise.'

She was clasping his hands in her own, imploring him by word and look. Her very soul seemed to be waiting upon his answer.

There was only one course for him to take.

'I promise, mother,' he said.

'On the word of a Percival — the promise which no Percival ever broke yet.'

There was only one course for him to take.

'I promise — on the word of a Percival,' he repeated; and, stooping, kissed her on the forehead.

'Leave me now, Duke; I am so tired.'

A week later she was dead.

11

HOPE DEFERRED

In the breakfast room of No. 8 Hamilton Terrace Harry Connor and his wife are seated at breakfast. The room itself is unchanged since we saw it on that Sunday morning in March; but instead of the elder Connor we have his son, and in the place of honour behind the teacups, where poor Mrs Connor used to preside, now sits the young mistress — once Julia Murphy.

Nora's place is vacant. She is breakfasting in bed, for she has not been very well lately, and this is what her brother and sister-in-law are now discussing.

'She has never been the same girl since Dad's loss,' said Harry. 'She felt it terribly — it was such a shock to her.'

'Yes, I know,' replied his wife, 'but all the same it's not natural for a young thing like her to take even such a calamity so much to heart. I believe the state of her health is to blame. I know she is not well, and she looks wretched. I intend to take her to Dr Mooney in a few days, if she is not better, and get his advice. Probably a tonic would put her all right.'

Julia Connor is much the same as was Julia Murphy — sensible, good-hearted, and matter-of-fact. If marriage has changed her at all, it is but to give her an added dignity and a greater amount of self-confidence, a quality in which she was never very seriously lacking.

'All right, my dear, whatever you think best,' assented her better half, who always put great faith in her judgement. After a minute, he added thoughtfully, 'I only hope that she is not by any chance fretting over that Percival fellow. I always knew that he was no good; I told my poor mother so, but, of course, she would not listen to me.'

'Oh, Nora has quite forgotten him,' said Julia. 'But I

must say that I was never so surprised in my life at anything
as I was at the way she took it when he went off with
himself. And I thinking all the time that she was madly in
love with him.'

Her husband stirred his tea absently, and then turned his
attention to his plate; but his manner was queer. It seemed
that he wanted to say something, but hesitated to do so.

'Well, what is it, Harry?' asked his wife, who could
read him like a book.

He did not speak for a moment. Then, looking her in the
face he said, in his slow, heavy way: 'I think he writes to
her.'

Julia sat up suddenly, almost upsetting her cup.

'Writes to her! that Percival bounder! Now, what on
earth makes you think that?'

'Several mornings when I happened to be down before
the post came I saw Mollie sorting the letters on the hall
table, and on each occasion she took one out addressed to
Nora.'

'Well?'

'Well, I asked her what she was doing with Nora's
letters. She got very red and confused, and stammered that
Miss Nora had asked her to bring her letters upstairs to her at
once.'

The morning post in the Connor household was left on
the breakfast table. Nora's correspondence consisted mainly
of letters from the nuns or her old school friends, which she
would read and comment upon as she took her breakfast.

But was it possible that she was receiving other letters —
clandestine ones? Julia's fine eyes narrowed as she pondered
the question.

'Why on earth didn't you speak of this before?' she cried
sharply. 'When was it that you saw these letters?'

'About two weeks ago was the first time, and then twice
since. They were all in the same handwriting — rather a
queer fist, too.'

Julia rose, and crossing to the old-fashioned bell rope,

rang it violently.

'What are you going to do?' asked her husband uneasily.

'Never you mind! You have muddled this affair long enough.'

Mollie, the trim, well-trained housemaid, entered.

'Did you ring ma'am?'

'Yes — I did. Shut the door and come here.'

The girl changed colour, but did as she was told.

'For how long have you been taking letters from the postman addressed to Miss Nora, and giving them to her secretly?'

A picture of guilt and confusion, Mollie stood gazing at her young mistress, whose eyes questioned her sternly.

As the girl did not reply at once, Julia made a bold move.

'You may as well speak the truth,' she said, 'because we know everything.'

Mollie, beginning to cry, sobbed out excuses. She had only done it to please Miss Nora; she never thought there was any harm in it; it was just a bit of fun, and so on.

'Did a letter come this morning?' interrupted Julia.

'Yes, one comes every day, ma'am.'

'Where is it? Has Miss Nora got it, yet?'

'No, ma'am. I was just going to take up her tray. Anne is making a bit of toast, and — '

'Where is the letter, then? Give it to me'.

With trembling hands Mollie produced it from some pocket. As she took it from the girl Julia said, coldly: 'you may go now. I will let you know later what I intend to do about this.'

Mollie left the room, her apron to her eyes, and Julia and Harry bent over the letter, turning it over in their hands, and inspecting it closely.

The writing was uncommon, and plainly that of an educated person; the envelope was of the best quality, and the postmark was that of a small town in the County Meath.

'I believe you are right,' cried Julia. 'It must be from that villain. Let us open it and see what he has to say for himself

— the brute!

Her fingers were already on the flap of the envelope, when her husband's big hand closed over hers, and took away the letter.

'No, my dear,' he said, in his slow, deliberate way. 'I open no letter that is addressed to another person, no matter who it is, and neither will I allow my wife to do so. This is the proper way to dispose of these epistles.' And as he spoke he flung the letter into the fire, hold it down with the tongs as it writhed and twisted in the flames.

'Harry,' cried Julia, tears of angry disappointment in her eyes. 'How stupid of you! You should have read that letter, it was your duty to do so! Then you would have known how far matters had gone between them!'

'There is no need to do that,' he replied. 'Because, no matter how far they may have gone, they go no farther now! I'll lock the letter box in future and keep the key, and every single one of these letters that comes will go into the fire! My fine gentleman will soon get tired when he finds no answers coming to his epistles.'

'But Nora will write to ask him why he is not writing?'

'Yes, at first she will, and those letters must not be posted. We shall have to find some way to prevent it. She hasn't been out of the house for the last few days, so if she's in the habit also of writing every day, like his lordship, Mollie must have posted them for her.'

'Leave Mollie to me!' replied Julia grimly. 'She will meddle no more in this matter — you may be sure of that. Thank God, we have found out the mischief in time!'

'Aye, thank God!' echoed her husband. 'The bounder! to think that he could treat my sister in that fashion, playing fast and loose with her! However, it is ended now!'

Mollie was called again, and told that she would not be discharged; another chance would be given her. But she must say nothing—nothing whatever—to Miss Nora about what had taken place that morning. When she took up the breakfast tray with Nora's breakfast, which was now ready, she was simply to say that no letters had come that morning.

'And there will be no more letters any day in future,' said her master grimly. 'And all you will have to do is to say that there is no letter when Miss Nora questions you. There is no letter, you understand? Just that and nothing more.'

'And another thing,' added Julia, 'no letters which Miss Nora may give you are to be posted until I have first seen them — I or the master. And don't forget this, Mollie! I suppose you don't want to be sent home to your mother without a character?'

'Oh, no, ma'am! Oh! indeed, you may depend on me in future. Oh, I'll be very careful, sir!'

We must remember that all this happened many years ago, when one could dismiss a servant and replace her easily and at once, just as one could leave a house that did not suit, and go for a stroll around all those dwellings with 'To be Let' signs staring from their gates or windows, and so choose whatever other dwelling seemed most suitable. Such a state of things seems almost incredible today, but it was true enough in the nineties.

Mollie, having hastily banished all signs of weeping and disorder from her face, entered Nora's room with the tray.

Nora was awake, had been awake for some time, wishing for her morning cup of tea, for she had a slight headache and had not slept well.

'Aren't you late, Mollie?' she asked, as the girl drew a little table beside her bed.

'Yes, Miss Nora. I waited for a bit of toast Anne was making for you. She thought you might fancy it.'

Nora sat up in bed and, leaning towards the tray, stretched out her hand to take Duke's daily letter, which was always brought her by Mollie on the mornings when she was not down early.

She did not see it and looked questioningly at the girl, thinking that she still had it in her pocket.

'There's no letter today, Miss Nora.'

For a moment Nora stared at her incredulous.

'No letter! Oh, but Mollie, there must be! Go down and look in the box again; you have missed it, and it will be seen; go quickly!'

'There is no letter, Miss Nora. There is no letter this morning.'

Parrot-like she repeated what she had been drilled to say. Then, fearing to remain longer, she left the room, saying that Anne wanted her. And Nora, left alone, lay still and stared at the ceiling of her blue and white room, wide-eyed and incredulous. No letter! There was no letter from Duke! For the first time since he had parted from her and gone to Belmont he had left her without her daily love letter. It was October now, the second week in October — five weeks since he had left her; on every day of those five weeks she had received a letter from him. He must be ill, or perhaps his mother was worse — or dead. Anyway, he would write tomorrow — that was sure! How foolish she was to be so worried just because he had missed one day. She poured out some tea and drank it feverishly, but Anne's toast remained untasted. Her headache seemed worse, and the thought of any food sickened her. Presently there was a knock on the door and her sister-in-law entered.

'Well, Nora, how are you this morning? Did you get your breakfast all right? Why, girl dear, you are eating nothing!'

Julia's sharp eyes were searching her face, wondering how she had taken the disappointment over the letter.

Nora flushed.

'I have a headache,' she said. 'And I'm not hungry. I'll be better presently when my headache goes away.'

Julia's heart was very tender towards this girl, whom she regarded almost as if she were a child — a child, too, who had to be protected just now.

'Don't get up at all if you don't feel quite well,' she said.

'Oh, I think I'll get up. I would rather be up!' was the quick nervous answer.

But as Julia left the room she carried with her the thought

of a pair of sad grey eyes and a pale worried face.

After all there was no question of getting up for Nora. Her headache became worse, and she developed a bronchial cold and a high temperature. Old Dr Mooney was called in, the genial family physician who had attended her in all her childish ailments. He felt her pulse, and patted her hand, and told her that she must be a good child and take her medicine and plenty of milk and soup, and that she would soon be quite well again.

Nora assented dully, and did all that they wished, but she spoke very little, and would lie for hours staring at the ceiling and the walls of her room, seeing nothing, but eating her heart out because Duke had not written.

She wrote to him three times, but when no reply came to her third letter she did not write again. She was as proud as she was sensitive, and now felt hurt to the quick; she argued that he must have got her letters, and even if his mother were worse or had died, surely he could have written, if it were but two lines!

Julia, watching her, and seeing how the lovely eyes became sadder and more wistful as the days passed, felt really sorry for her. But both she and Harry were sure that in a little time she would forget this man who, as they thought, was only amusing himself by a flirtation which would never come to anything, and could only prove a heartbreak for the girl. So they considered that they were but doing their plain duty towards her, when morning after morning they put Duke's letters in the fire, and also poor Nora's three, which Mollie — with a wholesome fear of dismissal and her mother's wrath always before her eyes — had obediently handed to them.

After seven days no more letters came from Duke for nearly a week. Then he wrote twice, and after that not again.

In the meantime both Nora and the Connors had seen in the papers the notices of Lady Percival's death. When no letter came then, Nora began to lose heart completely, and also to lose her faith in Duke. He had always said that if his mother died he would at once make their marriage public; and now Lady Percival was dead, and not only had he failed to keep his promise but he had ceased writing altogether. Cut to the quick, wounded to the very depths of her being, Nora resolved that, on her part, she would write no more, or make no further efforts of any kind to bring him to her side, if he did not care to come of his own free will. But what she suffered during this time of secret sorrow affected both her physical and mental health. She lost her interest in everything — except the one thing that gnawed at her heart by day and night. She seemed to have become older suddenly; it was as though a very sad and tired woman had taken the place of the schoolgirl with her laughter and childlike ways. Nora, the gay and innocent girl, had gone — never to return.

She tried to be like her old self before her brother and his wife, never dreaming for a moment that they knew the cause of her suffering; but it was not possible for her to play the part, and as day after day went by, and she recovered neither her health nor her spirits, the other two decided that she must go away for a change. Dr Mooney, too, thought that this would help her to get back to normal again. He did not, nevertheless, look upon her case as being a serious one — she was 'run down' and wanted a change of air and plenty of nourishment.

Julia mentioned the matter to Nora one evening, when the three of them were sitting at the dining-room fire.

'And we were wondering if you would like to visit the Byrnes again?' she said. 'You seemed to enjoy your time there last summer.'

But Nora shrank back as if the other had struck her. To go there, where every memory would conjure up visions of last August — to be within a few miles of Woodside Cottage, and all that it meant to her!

'Oh! no, no!' she cried, 'not there!'

Julia stared at her in frank surprise, but Harry said soothingly. 'Well! where would you like to go — eh, old girl? Choose for yourself; we don't mind. But I can't have my little sister going about looking like a ghost any longer!' For a moment Nora was silent.

'I would like to go and stay for a while with Aunt Delia,' she said then. 'It's so quiet out there near the hills, and I'd love to see all the animals again, and Charles Stewart — I want to feel his soft nose in my hand and look into his eyes, because they are so honest and true. Oh! Harry — let me go to Aunt Delia's.'

Tears welled in her eyes as her brother put his arms gently round her.

'Why, of course, girlie. You shall go to Aunt Delia if you like — why not? I'll drop a line to her this very minute, and if she gets it in the morning she can call for you at once.'

Evidently Miss O'Connor did get the letter in time, for the following day, about three o'clock, her old pony trap, with Kitty, the ancient and obstinate jennet, between the shafts, drew up before No. 8 Hamilton Terrace, and Aunt Delia herself, shabby as ever, ascended the steps and rang the bell.

She was shocked when she saw Nora; her niece seemed years older. She looked pale and thin, and as Miss O'Connor expressed it in her own mind, 'dead in herself'.

But Nora was genuinely glad to see her aunt, and showed more interest in her coming visit than she had shown in anything else since her illness.

Miss O'Connor would not stay a minute longer than she could help at Hamilton Terrace, for they had a long drive before them, and the evenings were short and cold, now that the end of October was drawing near.

Mollie was sent to carry Nora's suitcase to the trap, and Nora accompanied her, as she wanted to speak to the girl.

'Mollie,' she said, flushing and paling nervously, 'if — if any letter should come you will post it on at once? won't you, Mollie?'

'Oh! yes, yes, Miss Nora! I'll not forget!' stammered the girl, and fled back to the house muttering, 'May God forgive me!' under her breath, as her master and mistress with Miss O'Connor came down the steps.

Nora took her seat in the trap. Aunt Delia got in opposite to her and jerked the reins until Kitty was persuaded to move. Then they were off, jolting noisily along the Rathgar Road in the direction of Rathfarnham. Five minutes later from the opposite direction there came an outside car, on which was seated Duke Percival.

It also stopped before No. 8 Hamilton Terrace, and Duke jumping off, sprang up the steps to the front door, and pulled vigorously at the bell.

12

THE PRICE THE WOMAN PAYS

'CHARLES STEWART' was stretched full length before the porch of Mount Rosemary, Miss O'Connor's house, on the morning after Nora's arrival there. His long slender nose — one of the marks of his aristocratic lineage — was between his paws, and his eyes — those honest, faithful eyes so typical of his breed — were fixed on the door which led into the square hall, while his great feathery tail waved slowly from side to side as he listened for a step within.

Then the door opened and Nora appeared. In an instant the dog was on his feet, and with one spring landed his two paws on her shoulders, while he tried, by look and gesture, to tell her how glad he was to see her, and that he hoped she would soon get quite well, and stay and keep him company for a long time.

Nora patted him gently on the back and hugged him round the neck by way of assuring him that she, too, was glad to see him and that love for him had been one of her reasons for coming to Mount Rosemary. And then, in complete understanding, they strolled down the garden path together.

Mount Rosemary was a very old house. The square hall was used by Miss O'Connor as a sort of living room, and also as a receptacle for all kinds of odds and ends; bran, cats, poultry, food, eggs, flower seeds, fishing tackle, were all jumbled together along with old books and newspapers, garden tools and boxes. There were two other sitting rooms which she seldom used, and off these, three bedrooms. The house was built in bungalow style, all the rooms opening off each other, and no upstairs or downstairs.

In summer it was a delightful spot, with a rambling old

garden of fruit and flowers, all growing side by side. As a child Nora used to think that she was in fairyland itself when she was walking between Aunt Delia's raspberry and currant bushes. The big golden raspberries were her favourites; she much preferred them to the red variety, and she was especially fond of one bush which grew beside a big rose tree. The scent of the roses and the flavour of the luscious berries made a delightful jumble in her childish mind.

Miss O'Connor's roses were beautiful; nowhere else could be found in richer profusion the queen of all flowers. Everywhere through the garden were great bushes of cabbage roses and the real old fashioned moss rose; against the wall grew the Gloire de Dijon, while various others of every colour ran riot all over the garden.

The garden itself would have been the despair of a professional gardeners heart. Had Lady Percival or her Scotsman seen it they would have pronounced it hopeless. But it had a charm and fascination all its own, as have all these old gardens where nature is allowed a good deal of her own way, and the flowers and shrubs have liberty to grow as they please, and are not clipped and pruned and trimmed into shape by their owners.

On this fine day of late autumn there were only a few monthly roses left to grow side by side with the dahlias and chrysanthemums, and the Michaelmas daisies of soft blue. But, in the orchard behind, the apples were ripening on the trees, and the fig tree at the side of the house was laden with fruit.

The sun was shining brightly, the air pure and invigorating, with that intangible strengthening quality which the air of the Dublin mountains always seems to possess in an extraordinary degree; and Nora, as she stood in the garden and inhaled great breaths of it, felt better already in every way.

She had wanted to help her aunt with the breakfast, but the lady had brusquely informed her that she would only be in the way, and that she was to take herself off until the meal was ready.

And, after a while, Miss O'Connor came to the porch and called her in.

Breakfast was ready in the kitchen. Miss O'Connor, living alone and keeping no maid, usually had her meals there. The kitchen was big and sunny, and looked out on a grass plot, which was separated from the poultry yard by a wooden paling. Needless to remark, sundry persevering hens always managed to make their way through this paling, and in the springtime the chickens could never be kept out. Little fluffy chickens inside on the grass, and an hysterical mother on the outside, were always associated in Nora's mind with springtime at Mount Rosemary. Even this morning her aunt was vigorously 'shooing' at a little hen which had just taken a daring leap on the breakfast table. They were great pets, and each one had a name to which Aunt Delia always said it answered.

'Be off now, Mrs Rufus!' she cried. 'What impudence you have, to be sure! Here, Charles Stewart — come and chase her!'

With playful leap and apologetic bark — for he was the most gentlemanly of collies, and hated to hurt the feelings of any lady, even if she was only a hen — the big dog succeeded in sending Madam Rufus back to her own grounds. A couple of pet pigeons were strutting on the flagged floor, waiting to be fed, quite at home with Charles Stewart — upon whose beautiful coat they sometimes alighted — and also with Captain John, an immense grey cat, which was purring loudly on the sunny window-sill.

To Nora it seemed strangely peaceful and refreshing. Here, amongst happy memories of her childhood years, in this house where she had always been so happy — here she felt that she could be a girl again. She had slept last night, too — slept well for the first time in many weeks — in the white bedroom where the lattice window looked out on the Dublin hills. Always she had loved the mountains; summer after summer she had spent at Mount Rosemary, in preference to going anywhere else, for her greatest joy as a child had been to visit Aunt Delia. And now, when she carried a woman's sore heart, when she was weary with trouble and sorrow, she had come there for healing and strength.

And, for the first few weeks, it indeed seemed that she would soon be quite herself again. Harry and Julia, coming out to spend Sunday, were delighted with the improvement in her health and spirits.

Harry on this occasion took the opportunity of confiding in Aunt Delia about Duke Percival. She remembered him vividly on the afternoon of Mrs Connor's 'At-Home', when Nora introduced him, but she had not happened to meet him since. She was furious when she heard that he had been trifling with Nora — carrying on a flirtation, which could end in nothing but heartache for the girl when he got tired of it. So Harry Connor believed it, and no one, in the circumstances, as he knew them, can blame him for doing so. Miss O'Connor agreed with him, and heartily approved of what she called his 'plan of campaign'

'And you tell me that Nora and I had only just gone, the other day, when he drove up. Well! I declare to goodness, but that was a near shave!'

'Most providential,' replied her nephew. 'Looks to me, Aunt Delia, as if the Lord was on our side, anyway!'

'And you didn't interview him at all?'

'No. Julia luckily caught sight of him through the window. I made up my mind at once. We told Mollie to say that we were not at home. Of course, he asked for Nora first, and the girl told him that she had gone away for some time, and that she did not know her address. He seemed in a terrible way, and said he would come back again.'

'And did he?'

'Yes, late that night. We expected him, and put out the lights, and went to bed early. He knocked three or four times and then went away.'

'And then?'

'He called the next day twice, but Mollie told him that we had all gone away earlier that morning, and expected to be some months absent. She could not let him have the address, as she had orders to give it to no one. He tried very hard to get from her, even offering her a five pound note — a bribe which, I am afraid, would have gained him what he sought, if we had really been away.'

'Has he called again?'

'Good lord, yes! Nearly every day, sometimes alone, and sometimes with that friend of his — Vane, I think is his name. It's a blooming nuisance, Aunt Delia: I can tell you that, because both of us—and especially Julia, for she is more at home—are afraid he will catch us some day, or meet us out of doors.'

'Well! You will only have to be careful. And after another while he will give up the game. Mark my words; he will soon grow tired, when he finds himself up against a blank wall every time.'

'She has not posted any letters from here, I suppose?' asked Harry, lowering his voice, as Julia and Nora came in from the garden.

'No. You may make your mind easy on that score. She has not been beyond the garden, except when I have been with her; and the nearest letter box is nearly a mile away.'

At the end of three weeks, Duke, in despair, gave up calling at Hamilton Terrace, and the Connors breathed freely once more. It had been like a time of siege for them, and only for most careful planning on their part, and drilling of both Mollie and Anne — who both now looked upon Duke as a villain deeper than any of those that they had watched, with bated breath, walking the boards of 'The Queen's' — they would surely have had to meet him face to face. Not that either Harry or Julia would have minded that. Julia, especially, would have rather enjoyed giving him what she called 'a piece of her mind'. But they were anxious to get rid of him quickly and permanently; and they believed that a policy of dead silence — no letters, no information, no means of tracing Nora — Mollie having given him to understand now that she had gone to England — that all this would be the best and most effectual way to put off this man, whom they bitterly blamed for bringing such pain into the young life that was so dear to both of them. Little did they even dream of the true state of affairs. By their own misguided plans they had made it impossible for the facts to become known to them.

Towards the middle of November Nora returned to Rathgar. The days were foggy and cold, and Mount Rosemary, in the winter, was a very different place from Mount Rosemary of the sunny summer time. Also Julia felt that Nora might safely return now, for a few days previously she had read in the paper that Duke Percival and Jack Vane had volunteered for active service in South Africa, and were already on their way to join the British forces there.

'And a good end to bad rubbish, I call it!' declared Anne, as she and Mollie sat by the kitchen fire that night reading the same paragraph.

'Ah! but after all, he was a grand young gentleman! The lovely face and the eyes of him! Sure, I used to hate myself for the lies I was after telling him!' And Mollie sighed romantically.

'The grand villain, yez mean!' cried the cook. 'I'd tear the same two eyes out of his scheming head wid me own two hands! But, then, sure, I know what men are! And it's meself has reason to do so, after burying two husbands!'

Aunt Delia got the newspaper several times a week, although since her beloved 'Chief' had died she had taken but little interest in politics. However, the Boer war aroused her interest, and her rebel soul was on fire again.

'God grant them strength to beat England, anyhow,' she said fiercely, the morning before Nora left her — 'I'd die happy if I saw John Bull defeated!'

She had already seen the paragraph referring to Percival, and it had inflamed her still more against him. Going to fight under the Union Jack! Well, after all, what more or better could be expected of him? Wasn't he a Cromwellian — seed, breed ánd generation? But she cut out the paragraph and carefully burned it. Not that she need have troubled to do so, for Nora never glanced at a newspaper—and the war had no interest whatsoever for her. That Duke would be concerned in it she never for a moment imagined.

Although Nora was looking the better for her time at Mount Rosemary, her state of health still worried Julia, and one day she insisted that she should go with her to see Dr Mooney. Nora seemed strangely averse from the idea, but was compelled to yield.

Arriving at the doctors house, they were informed that he was away from home, but that another medical man was doing duty for him. Julia was annoyed that it was not Dr Mooney, who knew Nora so well; but now that she was there, she resolved to see the other man.

While they waited their turn to go in to the doctor, several patients being before them, she was struck by Nora's white face and strange frightened expression. She was glad that she had made her come for advice; any one could see that the girl was not well.

Dr Wilson, who was doing duty for Dr Mooney, was a man of about forty, with clever, clear-cut features and keen piercing eyes.

Julia simply introduced Nora as her sister-in-law, and gave him a few details. The doctor listened quietly, and then put a few questions to Nora.

She answered him nervously and quickly, her colour coming and going.

But he only smiled at her, as he said, kindly: 'Well, now, I don't think you have any reason to be worried. Your state of health is very natural, under the circumstances, and you are young and strong. Tell me, now, my dear, how long have been married?'

Nora sat as if turned to stone, staring at him with tragic eyes.

'Come, come!' he said, with an encouraging smile, 'you

need not be at all alarmed. Just answer my question: how many months have you been married?' He spoke kindly and quietly, believing that he had a very nervous patient. And she was so young to be a wife already!

But Julia suddenly interposed with flaming cheeks and an angry note in her voice: 'You are making some queer mistake, Dr Wilson,' she said. 'This is Miss Connor. I am her brother's wife, but she is not married.'

Dr Wilson drew his brows together with a quick frown, and glanced sharply from Mrs Connor's angry face to Nora's fear-stricken countenance. Here, then, was tragedy stark and cruel — here where he had least expected it. But a doctor learns never to show his feelings, so he only said, quietly: 'Not married? You tell me she is not married?'

'No, certainly not,' replied Julia, sharply, 'altho' I don't see, doctor, what that fact has to do with you one way or another.'

The doctor was silent for a moment, and then he said, glancing at Nora and quickly turning his eyes away from her face: 'Perhaps your sister-in-law could explain to you. As for me, I would prefer that you should consult another doctor. Dr Mooney will be back in a week, and as he has been your medical adviser for some years you had better see him.'

'But, but, oh! Dr Wilson, what do you mean?' cried Julia, in a sudden panic of fear.

'If you will come this way for a moment.' He drew her to the other end of the large room and spoke to her in a low voice for several minutes. Nora could not hear what they said, not indeed that she had the slightest desire to do so. She sat like a carved figure, motionless and rigid, her slim hands clasped in her lap.

Then she heard Julia's voice, highly-pitched, full of a fear which she was striving to keep at bay.

'I don't care, doctor. I don't believe a word of it. The thing is impossible, I tell you — impossible! And Nora — Nora. If you only knew her — '

'Suppose we ask the young lady herself?' suggested the doctor.

'But to speak to her of such a thing — it's an insult! Still, I'll ask her — just to show you! Nora,' cried poor Julia, too distracted to consider her words, 'Nora, Dr Wilson thinks that— that you are going to have a baby! Oh! tell him how absurd it all is—how impossible! Tell him what you think of such an idea.'

No answer came. The silence was absolute, except for a clock on the mantelpiece, which to Julia seemed to be ticking so loudly that she vaguely wondered why the doctor did not stop it. Then Nora spoke: 'I think the doctor is right,' she said. Her voice was absolutely devoid of expression. She spoke as one who was making an ordinary remark of no importance whatever. Julia stood for a moment gazing at her in horrified amazement. She really did not believe her own ears, and had a feeling that she was losing her senses. Then she found Nora's eyes looking into hers, and the truth came to her. Trembling in every limb, she dropped into a chair which Dr Wilson pushed near her.

'Oh! my God,' she whispered, brokenly, 'My God!'

13

RED WAR

To those of us who have lived through the Great European War, the fight between Boer and Briton of over twenty years ago seems but a small thing. But to the people of South Africa and of Britain it was then an event of vast moment

England declared that the fighting would be over by the Christmas following the October when hostilities first commenced. Some of us remember similar prophecies about the speedy termination of the later war with Germany. Neither prediction came true, as we now know. When England realised that the Boers meant to put up a stiff fight the usual recruiting and propaganda work began. However, it was not until practically the last year of the war that Britain had to call openly for volunteers

Duke Percival did not wait for such a call. He believed that Nora, for some extraordinary reason of her own, had left him and fled to where he could not find her — what else could he think? There was the sudden cessation of her letters; no reply to those he had written; no reply, no notice whatever taken of the letters he had left at her house, or of the verbal messages which he had poured into Mollie's ears.

As for Mollie herself, he could not fathom her attitude; Vane, too, had been puzzled by the girl's manner, and had often said to Duke that he was sure she was only the tool of another person, and acting on instructions given her.

'But she says that all the family are gone to England, and that she does not know when they will be back. You surely don't expect me to enter the house and search it — do you ?' objected Duke.

'No. Still, I wouldn't label Nora as the false and fickle creature which you now consider she is. She may be entirely the victim of circumstances.'

'She could write.'

'What if she were watched and not allowed even to post a letter?'

'Bah! Don't talk such idiotic twaddle! As if any girl of ordinary intellect couldn't manage — some way or other — to post a letter! Besides, her people don't know that there is anything between us.'

'They may have found it out by this.'

'How could they? Whatever else I may think about Nora, at least I know that she would not break her solemn oath. And Pierre is absolutely to be trusted.'

'Absolutely. By the way, he is quite cut up over Nora's disappearance.'

'Yes, he was very devoted to her.'

There was a momentary silence between the two men, who were lingering over the dinner at Andover Mansions. Then Vane spoke, referring to what Duke had mentioned earlier in the evening: 'Well! I would say don't be in too great a hurry. Wait a while longer, Duke. Suppose a letter came from Nora clearing up all this misunderstanding — which I firmly believe it to be — and you had gone to the Transvaal, think of the time it would take to reach you, if it ever reached you indeed! Wait a month longer!'

'No! Not a week longer!' cried Percival, angrily. 'It is no good for you to try and take Nora's part. She has behaved abominably! Either she has tired of our marriage already, and believes it to be a mistake, or else she has allowed herself to be cajoled or bullied by her people. In either case she is not worth another thought of mine!'

But Jack Vane, as he glanced across at his friend's haggard face and weary eyes, knew that whether she was worth it or not the girl wife still possessed most of his thoughts. Duke knew it, too. His mental suffering at this time was greater than he had ever known in all his previous life; sometimes he felt that he would go mad if he could not forget the happy laugh and the girlish face of her who had walked in Eden with him for ten heavenly days. Then his mother's dying wish came back to him, and with a remembrance came the thought that here was a path which might lead to a merciful forgetfulness. Amidst the danger and excitement, amidst the allurement of the pomp and panoply of war, surely the memory of one girl's wistful face framed in a rose-covered casement, and the sound of her laugh, would become dim and faint.

So, a week after the above conversation saw Jack Vane and himself in London. Jack was being sent out as a special correspondent, and was genuinely glad of the chance, hoping thereby to make both fame and fortune on the field.

Pierre was left in charge of the flat in Andover Mansions, with full instructions as to the forwarding of all letters and of any news — even the slightest — which he might learn about Nora. He was to keep a sort of watch on the Connors' house, and let Duke know when they returned, whether Nora was with them or not, and any other details which he could glean. Duke would write from time to time as soon as he knew where to forward letters.

Pierre promised to attend faithfully to everything, but he first stipulated for a month's holiday at home in France. This Duke allowed him to take, and so the Frenchman was not in Dublin when Nora returned from Mount Rosemary, or doubtless he would have seen her.

When our two friends reached London that great city was in the throes of war fever. Every day saw fresh contingents of men off to the front, while bands played, and wives and mothers wept; saw recruiting bands marching through the streets, while the women admired and children cheered and tried to imitate their martial gait; speeches were being made i n the British Parliament, and huge sums of money voted. But we have seen it all — multiplied a thousandfold — in recent years; and except for certain differences in dress and manners there is little to choose between the two periods.

In the nineties instead of the modern VAD, with her bobbed hair and short skirt, her eternal cigarette and 'swank' they had a more romantic and sentimental young lady, who wore an imitation nurse's garb down to her toes, and a fringe which would have made a gollywog envious.

But human nature itself does not change, and the people of the British Empire in 1899, who sent their fighting men off to South Africa to the strains of:

'Dook's son,
Cook's son,
Son of a Belted Earl!'

were not a whit different from those of the present generation, who screamed 'Tipperary,' and 'Keep the Camp Fire Burning,' until one's very soul was sick of the doggerels.

Duke Percival and Jack Vane remained only a very short time in London — just long enough to purchase a few necessaries to take with them, and then they set sail for the Transvaal.

During their first few months there they soon became accustomed to the fatigue and hardship of their new life; and in spite of danger and discomfort they both were glad of the experience. Duke made a splendid soldier. He seemed not to know what fear was, the reason being that he scarcely cared whether he lived or died. No word had come from Nora, and Pierre had written to say that on his return from France he had carefully watched No. 8 Hamilton Terrace. Both Mr & Mrs Connor he had seen, going in and coming out of the house, but of Madam — chère Madame — not one little sign!

Duke's heart still ached intolerably for his young wife, and if at times, in the rush and fever of the campaign, there came spells of partial forgetfulness, he would only suffer the more deeply when he had time to remember, lying out on the cold veldt under the African skies.

In February, 1900 the British forces to which Vane and Duke were attached, were encamped near the Riet River, and here they were attacked by De Wet and his burghers. The two opposing forces were about equal in numbers — each between three and four hundred men — but the British, who were guarding a convoy, were without guns for the first two hours. They then received a reinforcement of cavalry and four Armstrong guns, and redoubled their efforts to drive the Boers from the position they had taken under cover of the mule waggons. De Wet was exceedingly anxious to capture this convoy, as he knew that the loss of the provisions would be a serious blow to Lord Roberts, who was expecting them. The battle raged until darkness fell, and ended by the Boers capturing sixteen hundred oxen and forty prisoners.

Among the prisoners was Duke Percival.

During the fight he had been wounded in the leg, a flesh wound only, but one that caused him much loss of blood and consequent weakness. When he felt faintness stealing over him, and when he realised that the Boers were gaining the action, he thrust his hand inside his tunic and drew out an envelope.

'Jack,' he whispered, 'take this and try to mail it to Nora. It is to tell her to make our marriage public. I feel that I should not have made her promise to keep silence in this matter. Promise me, Jack.'

'I promise, dear old chap, I promise. But don't give up — we will get out of this all right.'

Just then the Boers made a final desperate charge. Vane was flung backwards from his friend's side, and in the darkness and confusion he could not again find Duke. For some time he hung around having several narrow escapes from death and capture, but at last he had to give up hopes of discovering where his friend was. He was fairly certain he had been taken prisoner; and sick at heart, weary in body and soul, Vane turned his back on the scene of the late fight and crept along by the river in the direction where he believed the next British camp was. But that part of the country was unknown to him. He was very weak, his brain was benumbed, and, staggering on wearily, he took the wrong direction unknown to himself.

Presently he saw what he took to be the English camp, and tried to hasten his step, calling out as he drew near, so glad, so thankful was he to be within the lines of safety.

To his surprise a voice answered him in Dutch. He realised too late that he had mistaken a Boer camp for the English one, and suddenly — panic-stricken — he did the worst thing possible in the circumstances; he turned away and tried to run.

The next moment the rifle of the Boer sentry spat viciously through the darkness, and Jack Vane — true friend and true lover—dropped on the veldt with a bullet through his brain.

14

THE KEEPING OF THE OATH

And now, to go back to Nora, as she faced the tragedy of her womanhood, on that black day towards the end of November, 1899.

She hardly knew how she and Julia got home to Rathgar. Like one in a dream she found herself in the tram, seated beside a strangely quiet Julia, who paid the fare with mechanical precision, and stared in front of her with a face of stone. Nora, on her part, felt that her personality was changed; she seemed to be someone else, some other girl altogether. Not Nora Connor, the happy thoughtless school-girl, care free and laughter-loving — to the Nora Connor who had become Mrs Nora Percival on that lovely day in mid-August, when she stood beside Duke in the little hillside church.

Nora Percival — and she could not claim her husband's name! Instead of holding up her head with the proud dignity of an honoured wife, she must be abased to the very dust, as if she were, indeed, the thing of shame which the tongue of scandal would proclaim her.

When they arrived at Hamilton Terrace she went quickly upstairs and, locking the door, flung herself face downwards on the bed — the white bed with the crude bows of blue ribbon, in which she had awakened on that far away Sunday in March, and thought about the wonderful Prince Charming — Romeo of the red-brown eyes — who had come so suddenly into her life, never to go out of it again.

For he could never really go out of her life now. She might never see him again, but there would be another life — a little life which would keep his memory for ever in her heart. Not that she wanted to forget him: he was her husband, and she loved him — more deeply now than ever.

But, lying there in her cold bedroom as the daylight faded and darkness fell, she wondered—as she had wondered and puzzled so often, of late — what had happened to change him?

Why had he stopped writing? What reason could there be for his treatment of her? Could he have tired so quickly? Only a fortnight married. And how devoted and loving he had been! Could he really have changed in such a short space of time?

Or was it possible that it had been some gigantic mistake or misunderstanding? What, if he had not received her letters?

She wondered where he was now — whether he was still in Belmont, or if he had returned to town? For a brief moment she thought of going to Andover Mansions and inquiring for him. Pierre who had been so kind to her—if she could even see him. But almost at once she put the thought from her. Her whole soul recoiled from it. She felt that if she were never to see him again, she still could not force herself in any way upon his notice.

But she would write. She would write one letter to him now, telling him what the future held for her. And this she would do, not for her own sake, but for that of the little one, who must not be born in the shadow of disgrace. And surely then he would, at least, write in return — write and release her from the terrible oath which some inner voice now whispered that she should never have taken.

And he might do more than write. Surely he would come to her himself in answer to such a letter. Was not a husband's place by the side of his wife at such a time?

Nora had not been surprised at the doctor's verdict. She had partly expected it. But her own knowledge of her condition was almost entirely instinctive — the wonderful maternal instinct which lies dormant in every woman. Otherwise, she was as ignorant as a child. In those days the plain facts of life were never mentioned before unmarried girls. How often had Nora heard her mother answer: 'No nice girl speaks of such things, my dear,' when she had innocently asked some question touching on these matters.

She had married, knowing nothing of what married life meant — but she had married a man who understood and honoured her innocence. In his attitude towards his girl-wife in the first days of their marriage, Duke Percival had proved himself to be worthy of the trust and love which she had given him.

And, as she remembered him then, she felt more and more puzzled by his recent behaviour.

Anyway, she would write; she would direct the letter to Belmont, and surely then it would be forwarded to him wherever he might be. Then he would come to her — oh! yes, she knew he would come —and everything would come right then.

She rose from the bed and lit the gas. Then, catching sight of her reflection in the mirror, she gave a little cry of dismay, and pouring out water hastily, bathed her face and hands, and brushed her hair. Sitting down then, she drew her gay little blotting pad towards her, and dipping her pen in the ink, she was going to begin her letter, when she heard footsteps coming up the stairs, followed by a knock at the bedroom door.

She suddenly realised that she must have been some hours alone. Harry would be home from business. Julia would have told him, and now they must be coming to question her— to ask questions to which she could not reply. She thrust the note paper and ink quickly aside. The knock was repeated, but she did not move, and the door handle rattled impatiently. Then she heard her brother's voice: 'Open the door, Nora — at once,' and his words had a harsh, rasping sound, such as she had never heard in his voice before.

Rising slowly to her feet, she crossed the room and unlocked the door.

Julia and Harry came in, and as Nora saw her brother's face she shrank back from him. With stumbling step she reached a chair and sat down; but her wistful eyes still sought her brother — the brother who was gazing at her as if she had been a stranger within his gates.

He was pale and haggard; anyone looking at the man would have known at once that he had had a great shock of some kind. For a moment he did not speak; then he said: 'We have come to hear the truth from you about this — this terrible thing.'

Julia sat down at a little distance from Nora, but her husband remained standing, looking down at the sister of whom he had been so fond and so proud,

Nora did not speak; she could only look at him with a world of appeal in her childlike eyes.

'Come,' he repeated, impatiently. 'What have you to say?'

She moistened her lips.

'I have nothing to say,' she said then, her voice only a whisper.

'Nothing to say,' he shouted. 'Nothing to say! 'By God! I'll make you speak. Who is the man?'

Silence.

Stooping, he shook her, almost roughly — he, who had never spoken a sharp word to her all his life before.

'Tell me the name of that man!' he repeated.

'No, Harry. I will not — I cannot tell you.'

For the moment it almost seemed that he was going to strike her, but Julia, white-faced and troubled, went to the girl's side, and put her arm about her trembling form.

'Don't, Harry — don't be so rough with her!' she begged, the tears running down her cheeks. 'It's not her fault — sure she is just like a child! Don't hurt her!'

Harry turned away, and took a few strides up and down the narrow room, as if trying to regain his self-control. Julia drew the girl's head back on her shoulder, and kissed the white, drawn face. She had meant to be stern, to let her sister-in-law understand her own disgrace, and the shame which she had brought upon her family — that family to which Julia now belonged. But her love for the girl conquered her pride and anger, and now she felt only a tremendous pity for the little creature who lay like a bruised flower against her breast.

'Don't — don't be fretting, Nora, darling,' she said. 'It's not you we blame—but you must tell us who the man is.'

'I cannot — I cannot,' whispered the other. 'Don't ask me any more questions, please, Julia — for I can say nothing!'

'But, Nora — it is your duty. You must speak. Harry will be furious if you don't.'

'I can't help it, Julia.'

'But I say that you can and must speak,' cried Harry, wheeling round and standing in front of the two women. 'Tell me, at once, the name of this man.'

Then, as he saw that she made no attempt to answer him, he said more quietly, but with a stinging contempt in his voice, which cut her like a lash —. 'After all, there is no need for you to speak. We know who has been the cause of your ruin; we know who has dragged you through the mud, and then left you! It is that Percival cad, who was hanging around you all the summer.'

There was no need to seek further confirmation of their suspicions. One glance at Nora's scarlet face and quivering lips told them that they were on the right track. But the vivid flush faded almost immediately, leaving her paler even than before. Lifting her tired eyes to her brother's face — eyes, whose dark circles told of her weariness and pain — she said, 'I can tell you nothing — I can answer no questions.'

'Good God!' he shouted, furiously. 'Is it possible that you can still be my sister? Have I lived to see this day? The day when you have brought ruin and disgrace on us all! And then you refuse — absolutely refuse — to speak the truth about this cad, who first betrays you, and then goes off with himself to South Africa.'

South Africa! Did Harry say South Africa? Why that was where the war was — the Boer war, where all the fighting was taking place. War — war! What was that which the gipsy had said in the woods on that halcyon day of mid-August — their last perfect day together? 'A battlefield far away — miles and miles across the ocean.' Oh! but, surely, Duke wasn't there! Dear God! Was she going mad that she should even think of such a thing?

Forgetting all but her anxiety about the man she loved, she sprang from her chair, and seizing her brother by the arms, she shook him violently — although hardly conscious of what she was doing.

'What are you saying?' she cried, her voice shrill with fear. 'Harry! what do you mean about South Africa? You are trying to frighten me. Oh! you are cruel — cruel! Duke is not gone there! There — where they are fighting!'

'That is just where he has gone,' replied her brother, grimly. 'The newspapers announced his departure several weeks ago. And that will show you how much he thinks of you, or cares for you. You are ruined and disgraced — left with his child to proclaim your shame before the world — and he goes off to the Transvaal! But, as there is a just God in heaven, I swear I will make him pay for his sin yet! Heaven hear my oath!'

'Oh! don't — don't take an oath! An oath! Oh! God! an oath!'

The words had brought to her poor distracted mind the memory of the oath which she had taken — the oath the keeping of which would mean her present disgrace and that of her innocent child.

With a little moan her arms slipped to her side, and her brother just caught her in time as she was falling to the floor in merciful oblivion.

Julia was very kind to her that night. The memory of her sister-in-law's kindness to her during those terrible hours when she first realised that Duke was gone so far away always remained with Nora, even after she learned the part which Julia had taken in separating her from her husband. And she was particularly grateful to Julia because she did not ask her any more questions, or, indeed, talk at all to her, but just gently helped her to undress.

Then she called Mollie and told her to light a fire, as Miss Nora had got a bad cold. The girl was really shivering with misery and cold, and in spite of her mental torture she experienced a sense of physical relief when she was at last in bed, sipping some hot milk.

Julia left her then and went downstairs to her husband. They sat till long after midnight discussing this terrible tragedy that had befallen them.

There was so much in it which puzzled them. How and where had Nora managed to meet Duke Percival in secret? They had believed that they knew all about her movements during the last few months.

And then Julia suddenly thought of the visit which her sister-in-law had paid to the Byrnes in Wicklow during the previous August.

'Could it be possible,' she said to Harry, 'that Nora did not go there on the date arranged? Suppose she met this Percival and went somewhere with him first?'

'By Jove! I believe you've hit the right nail on the head,' he said. 'Write in confidence to Mrs Byrne, and ask her on what date Nora arrived at their place.'

But Julia shook her head.

'No,' she replied. 'I'd be afraid to arouse her curiosity, in case that — that she might hear anything later. And that reminds me, Harry, what are we going to do with her? Where can we send her? You know she cannot possibly remain here much longer.'

'I don't know of any place — except Aunt Delia would have her,' Harry said moodily, his expression plainly showing how distasteful the whole discussion was to him. 'She could stay there quietly until — until everything was over.'

'Yes — if your aunt would have her,' replied Julia meditatively. 'I wonder would she? If not, we will only have to send her to England. No doubt there are plenty of comfortable homes for such cases, as long as one pays well. But, if only Aunt Delia would have her, it would be the best. She could stay at Mount Rosemary, and not a soul would ever see her, or know that she was there.'

'Yes, but it would be dreadfully dull and lonely for Nora

— poor thing,' said Harry, doubtfully. He was already repenting of his harshness towards the little sister, who, he knew in his heart, must have been 'more sinned against than sinning'.

'Yes, I know,' assented his wife, adding, 'but what else can we do? We must keep the affair hidden, both for her sake and our own. Afterwards, she can return here, and as for the — the other — we will pay to have it minded somewhere.'

'There's another thing you may as well know,' said Harry suddenly. 'I'm going down to Meath tomorrow, to Belmont. I'll tell Sir Roger Percival, and get this cad's address, or find out where his letters are to be sent. Aye, and I'll tell the old man what I think of his precious son. The unspeakable ruffian!'

'What use would that be?' said Julia. 'I think it would be very foolish of you to go. What good could it do, anyway. You know perfectly well that they would never consent to his marrying Nora. They don't consider that anyone in our class is a suitable match for a Percival of Belmont.'

'Don't they, indeed?' Well, I'll soon show them what all decent people think about their Percivals of Belmont when they behave as low-down cads.'

'Anyhow, let us get to bed now, ' said Julia, wearily. 'God knows I'm tired enough! But I doubt if I shall be able to sleep. I'll write to Aunt Delia tomorrow; it would be well to have her advice, for she is very sensible, in spite of being such an oddity.'

They went upstairs, and together tip-toed into Nora's room. All was quiet. The girl seemed to be sleeping; on the pillow lay the little white face, the soft hair spread around, one slim hand pressed to her bosom. The firelight shone around the room, showing the photos of her favourite nuns and schoolfellows, and Harry's own photo, in the particularly smart frame which she had bought with her own pocket money. He glanced at it, and turned away sorrowfully to look at the bed. The lamp burning before the Madonna and Child shed its soft rays on his sister's face so pale and drawn; while every now and then, even in her sleep, a sob would break from her — as from a little child who had cried itself to sleep.

Julia's eyes filled with tears.

'Oh!' she whispered. 'To think that Nora — our dear little Nora —'

Harry's eyes were wet, too, as he slipped an arm round his wife and drew her towards the door. And as they stole softly from the room, they little dreamt that the hand which lay across Nora's breast was pressing her wedding ring close to her faithful loyal heart.

The next morning Julia herself helped to prepare a dainty breakfast tray, and was about to carry it upstairs, when she heard Harry calling her. Giving it to Mollie, she went into the breakfast room to see what her husband wanted; but she had not been long there before Mollie came rushing down the stairs and into the room, pale and frightened.

'Mollie! What is it?' cried Julia, an unknown dread filling her mind.

'Oh! ma'am — oh! Miss Nora is not above in her room. She's not in the bathroom, or anywhere, and her room is all upset. Her suit-case and other things are gone! Oh! Ma'am, and she so sick. What in the world has happened her?'

What, in the world, indeed — poor distracted soul!

15

PIERRE GREETS THE NEW YEAR

'And I suppose you bullied and brow-beat her! And frightened the life out of her — the poor darling! I declare to goodness it makes me sick to listen to the pair of you talking now, after you being the cause of her running from her home.'

Miss O'Connor was seated in the dining-room of No. 8 Hamilton Terrace, and Harry and Julia were seated opposite, feeling very like two culprits before a stern judge.

It was the afternoon of the same day on which Nora's disappearance had been discovered, and as soon as they realised that she was really gone, Harry had taken a car out to Mount Rosemary and brought Aunt Delia back with him. She had come prepared to stay a few days. The daughter of a neighbour, a sensible girl, who had minded the house and live-stock on previous occasions, had been left in charge at Mount Rosemary, and Aunt Delia, carrying a canvas bag stuffed with various necessaries, and accompanied by Charles Stewart, had come back with her nephew to Rathgar. She had at first hardly credited what they told her.

Doctors were fools — after all, what did even the best of them know? But after a while she was forced to believe them, and her weather-beaten honest face looked strangely grey and haggard as she listened to all they had to tell her. She was furious with Harry because he had spoken harshly to the girl, who was so dear to her withered heart. They had hidden nothing from her telling her all that had taken place the previous night, and adding how surprised they were at Nora's flight that morning, because she had been sleeping so quietly when they went into her room at a late hour.

'Pretending to sleep no doubt!' snapped Miss O'Connor. 'Wanted to get you out of the room — had had enough of the two of you already.'

'No, Aunt Delia,' interposed Harry. 'I know that she was really asleep, because every now and then she would give a little sob.'

'Which shows how she must have cried before she fell asleep from exhaustion. Really, Harry, I did not think that you had it in you to be such a brute.'

He flushed painfully, but said nothing, and on seeing his distress Miss O'Connor relented a trifle. 'Well,well,' she said, 'It's no use crying over spilt milk! What we have to do now is to get her home again as soon as possible. Is there any likely place where you think she would go?'

For hours they talked and planned and schemed. Julia was afraid to write direct to Mrs Byrne asking if Nora had gone there, but she wrote a friendly note just to find out all she could.

However, Mrs Byrne's reply, in which she spoke of Nora, and sent her her love, proved that she certainly had not gone to Wicklow.

They inserted advertisements in all the daily papers, carefully worded, but which they thought Nora would understand.

'She never reads the newspapers,' cried Julia.

'She will read then now,' asserted Miss O'Connor. 'She will get them to read the war news to see if there is any mention of Duke Percival.'

Aunt Delia understood her own sex. But no reply came to any of the advertisements, and no news of any sort could be got of the missing girl.

As yet they had not called in the help of the police, for they dreaded the publicity and scandal which would be sure to follow such action. But as day after day went by, and there was still no tidings they realised that they must let the police know. Hospitals were visited, and — most dreadful of all— the morgue. Sometimes in a frightened dream Julia would see Nora's still form lying on the stone slab, all wet and dripping from the waters of the Liffey, and she would waken Harry, with her agonised cries.

Aunt Delia spent much of her time at Rathgar, going home a few times every week to see if Mary Malone was doing the work of Mount Rosemary as it should be done. Charles Stewart always accompanied her there and back, but with the intelligence of his breed he had immediately sensed that something was wrong, and he spent many hours going up and down and through the house, nosing and smelling; and looking. And they all knew for whom he was seeking; but the days passed, and she was not found.

Early in December Harry went down to Belmont. Nora's flight had put all else out of his mind; he was so upset and distracted that he was afraid to go anywhere, or do anything in case he should miss her. His business was left to the care of the manager, and poor Harry spent his days searching here, there and everywhere, and yet fearing to do it openly — trying still to hide his sister's disgrace.

But on this day he determined to interview Sir Roger Percival, and see if he could obtain Duke's address from him. As to whether he would speak to the old man about Nora he was not yet decided on that question.

Asking the way from the station-master at the small country station, he walked swiftly in the direction of Belmont. It was a bitterly cold day, the sky dark and lowering. Arriving at the lodge gates he found them wide open, and the old woman of the lodge ran out and called out something — it was as if she was asking a question. But Harry took no notice of her, and striding up the splendid avenue where the trees today stood bare and leafless, and the old keep in the distance seemed to have such a ghostly appearance, he presently saw the big grey mansion looming in front of him. As he gazed at it, a great wave of hatred filled his soul — class hatred, racial hatred, and above all, hatred for the breed of those who had stolen his sister's honour.

'The cursed Cromwellians,' he muttered; and ascending

the great stone steps, he pulled the old-fashioned bell savagely.

The door was opened immediately by the butler, and engrossed though he was by his own trouble, Harry Connor could not fail to observe that the servant seemed strangely perturbed. Glancing over the man's shoulder into the interior of the long hall, he saw that it was full of men, talking and whispering, while an atmosphere of gloom and anxiety seemed to permeate the whole place.

However, what had all this to do with him? He had come there for a certain purpose and he would carry it out. He addressed himself to the butler.

'I want to see Sir Roger Percival,' he said curtly.

The butler looked astonished, and for a moment did not reply. Then —

'Sir Roger is seeing no one today sir,' he said.

'But I must see him — I insist on doing so.'

A tall dark man, with 'medico' writ large upon him, came forward.

'I do not know what your business may be,' he said to Harry, 'but you cannot possibly see Sir Roger today. Mr Everard Percival met with an accident in the hunting field a few hours ago, and he has just succumbed to his injuries.'

Harry Connor stared at him stupidly.

'Do you mean that he is dead?' he asked.

'Yes, he has just passed away. It has been a terrible shock to Sir Roger, who has not been strong since the death of her ladyship. I am sure you will now understand and leave your business for a later date.'

Without another word Harry turned and went down the steps, and through the avenue, and so out on to the bare country road beyond that led back to the station. Rain — cold as sleet — was falling, and the deepening dusk seemed a fitting atmosphere for the great house of mourning he had left behind — the house whence the heir had gone forth that morning, strong and vigorous, full of the joy of life, and where he lay now stiff and cold in death.

Harry Connor, in spite of the cause which he thought he

had for hating the whole house of Percival, could not but feel a vague pity for the broken old man in his lonely mansion. And that reminded him that Duke was now the heir, and would in course of time, if he survived the war, become Sir Duke Percival. He ground his teeth in sudden rage and vowed once again to make this man pay for what he had done.

He tramped moodily to the station, wondering from the depths of his suburban soul, how anyone could care to live in the country, and thought gratefully of No. 8 Hamilton Terrace, with the electric lamp shining outside the gate, and the clang of the passing trams.

After a week he wrote briefly to Sir Roger, simply inquiring as to where letters might be sent to Duke. He received a curt note in reply, informing him that Mr Duke Percival was at present with Her Majesty's forces in South Africa, that all letters were to be sent to him addressed — Expeditionary Forces, Johannesburg, but that as he was on active service, when he would receive them must be uncertain.

Harry wrote a scathing letter to Duke, but he did not mention in it that Nora had disappeared. And so time went on and there was still no trace of her. The police had accomplished nothing, and to excuse their want of success, they put the blame on Harry because he did not let them know about it from the first. They said valuable clues had doubtless been lost through such negligence.

***

All this time Pierre Lamont had been keeping a vigilant watch on the house in Hamilton Terrace, and on several occasions he had been sorely puzzled. Something seemed to be wrong; Miss O'Connor was constantly going in and out and looked haggard and worn. The young couple also looked ill with worry, and Pierre had seen the servants with tears in their eyes talking to men at the door. Detectives these appeared to be, as Pierre observed them keenly. But of Nora, as he had written to his master, 'there was not one little sign'.

He could only continue to watch and wait. His beloved master, so far, was safe and well, and wrote to Pierre when he could. Mr Vane had managed to keep with him, and even in the firing line they were together. Although, as Pierre knew, Jack was not a soldier, still these two friends would stick together as long as they could; separation was the only thing that they dreaded.

And in all Duke's letters came the question —'*Any news of Madame? Do you never see her?*'

Pierre would have gladly given several years of his life to be able to send news of good import across the seas.

And so the days passed, weary, pain-filled days for the Connor family. And for the first time in all her life Nora was away from home when the Christ Child came on earth.

When New Year's Day dawned, Pierre looked out of the window of 29 Andover Mansions, and saw that the morning was bright and frosty, the sky clear overhead and the ground hard and dry.

He experienced a sudden desire to go into the country; to get away from the city even for a day; to walk between red-berried hedgerows where the robins would be singing 'bon jour! bon jour!' on this the great feast day of his beloved France. He took a ticket, haphazard, to Greystones, and when he left the train at that station he started off to walk into the country. He strode along for several miles on the quiet country roads, where his feet rang out on the frozen ground and the little robin redbreasts, just as he had pictured, peeped out boldly at him from the hedges, singing, 'bon jour! bon jour, monsieur,' looking just as if they were birds on a Christmas card.

About two o'clock he began to feel hungry. He had brought some sandwiches with him, but nothing to drink, for being a great coffee-drinker he had hoped to find some place where he could get his favourite beverage. Had he known Ireland better he would have understood how unlikely it was that he would be able to procure any drinkable coffee in a roadside cottage.

But he did not know this, and so walked on, keeping a sharp look-out. Presently half a dozen labourers' cottages came into view. He knocked at the first door, which was opened by a slovenly woman, and gazing beyond her he saw an interior of dirt and disorder and screaming children, to say nothing of two dogs and several hens. Making some excuse, he turned away, and although some of the other cottages seemed cleaner he did not venture again, but walked further up the road in the hope of some better place appearing.

And sure enough he presently descried, standing by itself and surrounded by a stout hedge, a tiny thatched cottage. White curtains hung in the shining windows, the blue smoke of a turf fire ascended sky-wards, and lo and behold, a card inscribed with the words *Teas served here* hung in the window.

To see such a card displayed in such an out of the way spot, and in the depth of winter, surprised Pierre. But he was hungry and tired and very cold. Hot coffee would be delightful, and if tea — then why not coffee? At least he could try, and swinging open the little gate he knocked at the door. It opened almost at once and a girl stood before him.

'Pardon, mademoiselle,' began Pierre, sweeping off his cap, 'but I understand' — he stopped suddenly, silenced, and stood as if turned to stone, gazing wide-eyed at the girl, who was staring back at him, white-faced and wondering.

For a moment neither spoke. Then she said, with a sob sounding through the gladness of her voice — 'Oh, Pierre! dear Pierre! Is it really you?' And she reached out both her hands to him.

'*Mon Dieu! madame! Ah chere madame!*' cried the little Frenchman, and lifted her hands to his lips.

16

CAN SPRING BE FAR
BEHIND?

Nora told Pierre her story later, as they sat by the turf fire in
the tiny living room of the cottage. The Frenchman's
beloved coffee was steaming on the table beside him.
Noticing how cold and tired he looked, Nora started to make
him some at once, but he took the task out of her hands, and
made the coffee himself — as only one of his race can make
it.

And then he did not wish to sit at the table with Nora.
Would not madame drink a cup first? He could have some
afterwards. But she laughed at him — so glad she was to see
a friendly face once more — and insisted that they sit down
together at the small table in front of the turf blaze. But,
although they drank the coffee, they were too excited to eat.

She told him everything that had happened since she had
last seen him; and what a story it was for Pierre to sit and
hear! At times it seemed that he was almost choking — that
he would have to speak.But, by a great effort, he restrained
himself from saying anything until Nora had finished
speaking.

'So, you see, Pierre,' she was saying, 'when I awoke
on that morning in November, and remembered the shame I
would bring upon my brother and his wife on account of the
oath I had taken — well, I just felt that I could not bear it. I
had quite given up all hope of hearing from my husband,
now that I knew he could go to South Africa and never even
say goodbye to me! But all the same I would keep my oath
until he released me from it, as I had promised him. But oh,
Pierre, the keeping of it meant the loss of so much and made
me appear to be so wicked. Of course he never guessed what

it would cost me — I know that. But I could not endure the thought of more questions and looks from Harry and Julia. Aunt Delia, too, would have to know; and I love her so much. So I got up that morning and lit the gas — it was not yet daylight — and dressed myself. Then I packed a few things in a suitcase and slipped downstairs as softly as I could, and got out of the house and away without wakening anyone. I took all the money I had with me. It was just twenty pounds; it was not often I had so much, but Harry had just given it to me to buy some winter clothes, and I had not touched it. I walked about the streets until it was light — oh, how wretched and cold and sick I felt! But I could not go back and face them all again.'

'Mon Dieu! Mon Dieu!' wailed Pierre, staring into the fire, and beating one hand against the other.

'I wanted to get away — quite away,' continued Nora, 'to some place where I would not be likely to meet anyone I knew. No one goes to Greystones in the winter, so I went to Harcourt Street and took a ticket for that place, and while I was waiting for the train I got some tea. When I got to Greystones I took a room in a house near the sea, but I did not like the landlady. She was very inquisitive, always asking questions and staring at me. And then her terms were very high and I was afraid to spend a penny more than I could help. So one day when I was out walking I found this little cottage. There was a notice that it was to be let furnished, and naming a shop in the village where applications for it were to be made. I inquired there and found that the rent was only two pounds a month at this time of year. So I took it and I have lived here ever since.'

But not alone, madame — alone in a place so *triste!*'

'Yes, quite alone, except for the big cat you see there. She walked in half-starved one cold night and has stayed ever since. But it has been lonely, Pierre — dreadfully lonely. Still, there are things which are far worse than loneliness. It is worse to see scorn and pity in the eyes of those you love — to be regarded by them as a bad woman.'

'Oh, madame, that you — you...!'

'Yes, Pierre, I know, and you know, that I am not what they think; but we know, too, that I cannot clear myself in their eyes. So I was glad to be here, hidden away. All I was afraid of was that my money would run short. No matter how careful I might be it could not last very long; a good deal of it is gone already. So I put that card in the window — and you are my first customer.'

'Ah, but dear madame, there is no need — not of the slightest — to worry about money. Oh, if monsieur but knew.'

'You have news of my husband? You have heard from him lately? Oh! tell me — tell me.'

And then he told her. He told her all that had happened; how Duke had had no letters from her since October; how he had written again and again; had come to Dublin and called many, many times at Rathgar, always to get the same answer — everybody was away, no one at home, and there was no address to which he could write.

As he talked and she remembered certain incidents — Mollie's strange behaviour at times and some remarks Julia had made — she realised the truth. They must have intercepted all letters, and, while she was at Mount Rosemary, foiled all his attempts to find her again. But the anger which she felt against her people was almost forgotten for the moment, in the overwhelming joy which it brought her to know that her husband still loved her, and had always been true to her. For Pierre had painted for her very vividly, the picture of the anguished, distracted Duke as he went daily to Hamilton Terrace, and wrote letter after letter to which there was never a reply.

'Sorrow drove him to the war, madame. It was that he wished to forget, for he thought madame had forgotten him.'

'As if I could ever forget him — my dear husband! Oh!, Pierre, how could he think so? But thank God that he loves me still,' she whispered, the tears running down her face; 'and it was God sent you to me today — on New Year's Day. Oh, Pierre — a happy New Year to you, and to us both.'

'*Mais oui*, madame — a happy New Year, indeed. You will write to monsieur — is it not so? — and I also write — and when he gets the letters — behold, how quick he will return, and all will be happiness and joy. But, in the meantime, madame cannot stay here; it is not fitting for Madame Percival — Monsieur has left me in charge, and so madame will return with me to the flat of monsieur, where I, Pierre Lamont, will make her so comfortable until the return of monsieur.'

'Oh, Pierre!' she cried, half laughing, half crying. All these past weeks she had been so lonely, and yet she had never felt afraid. It had been a mad thing to do — to run away from home and to take this cottage, in the heart of the country almost, for there was no other dwelling nearer than the labourer's house which Pierre had passed half an hour before he reached Nora's abode. And yet, she had never felt fear, not even in the long winter nights when the daylight faded so early and she and the big cat would sit, one on each side of the turf fire. She would say her Rosary kneeling there, night after night, and pray. Oh, how she prayed! Only the dear Mother of God herself knew what fervent petitions went up to heaven for Duke's protection and safe return. Then she would go early to bed, and every day went out for a good walk, sometimes further into the country, and sometimes into the village of Greystones — a small, quiet place then — for anything she needed. And she looked well. There was a colour in her cheeks and her eyes were bright.

But at first she shrank from the thought of going to Duke's flat, and it took Pierre some little time to persuade her. He did so at last, however, and once he had got her consent, he insisted that there was no time like the present, and induced her to return with him that evening. On their way they left the key of the cottage with its owner, and then took the train to Dublin, the girl carefully carrying the cat which had been her only companion for so long. And for the first time since her marriage, Nora slept that night beneath her husband's roof. With mingled feelings of joy and pain she went from room to room, touching each intimate object that reminded her of him, laying her cheek against the cushions of the armchair where his dear head must have often rested.

Pierre was beside himself with delight. Had she been a queen he could not have treated her with greater honour. For her he composed his daintiest dishes; the lightest omelettes, the most delicious cakes, were always ready, and he seemed to think that she ought to take coffee or soup every hour.

But as the weeks passed and no answer came from Duke to their letters, both began to feel very worried and anxious.

Then one morning in March, the morning paper had a paragraph about the fight near the Riet River, and mentioned that Mr Jack Vane, war correspondent, was reported missing and was believed to have been killed; also that Mr Duke Percival, son of Sir Roger Percival, of Belmont, in Co. Meath, had been wounded and taken prisoner by the Boers.

Pierre coming into the library with her breakfast tray — for she liked to have it there, sitting by the fire in Duke's chair — found her lying on the hearth-rug, the newspaper clutched in her hand. She was very ill for days afterwards. The medical man who was called in that morning by the distracted Pierre, asked if the lady had no mother or sister who could come to her at this time. The Frenchman simply said that her husband was at the war, and gave no further details. Nora, hearing what the doctor said, asked weakly for her Aunt Delia. 'Don't bring anyone else, Pierre, but I would like Aunt Delia.'

The doctor sent in a nurse, and Pierre started off to Rathgar. On inquiry at Hamilton Terrace he was informed that Miss O'Connor was at Mount Rosemary. Hailing an outside car he gave the address to the driver, and they set off to Rathfarnham and thence on to the Whitechurch Road beyond.

It was a blustering day in March, but the skies were blue overhead and signs of spring were everywhere; the hedges were shooting into green, the violets were hiding here and there, and one or two early primroses were leading the way for the rest. The daffodils were blooming in the porch at

Mount Rosemary, where Aunt Delia was standing, feeding her first clutch of chickens, when the car drove up. As Charles Stewart gave his deep bark she turned her head and saw Pierre Lamont at the gate.

He was, of course, quite unknown to her, and going forward she asked what he wanted.

Pierre bowed and raised his hat.

'Pardon if I mistake,' he said, 'but is it that I address Mademoiselle Connaire?'

'My name is Delia O'Connor, young man, if that is who you are looking for?' And as he bowed in assent, she added — 'Well; what do you want?'

He told her as well as he could, she standing and staring at him, almost speechless between surprise and anger. But she found her tongue at last.

'So you are in league with that other ruffian, I suppose?' she foamed. 'I declare to goodness that if I had a horsewhip handy, I'd try to lay it across your back, old as I am.'

The Frenchman stared at her, not comprehending; and as Miss O'Connor continued to look at him, she was surprised to find herself thinking that, in spite of all, this man had a good face, honest and sincere, with eyes that looked at her frankly.

'Do not be angry, mademoiselle,' he begged; 'I know that to you things must appear of the blackest. But they are not so. It is not possible that I say more. Come with me — I beg you. Mademoiselle Nora is very sick — she cries for the Aunt Delia!'

'All right — I'll come with you. Just wait till I tie on me hat! But mind, wherever I go Charles Stewart goes too!'

Pierre glanced round for Charles Stewart in some perplexity, but saw no one except the big collie which was standing beside him, wagging his feathery tail.

'I declare to goodness, you'd think he knew you. I never saw him so friendly with a stranger before,' exclaimed Miss O'Connor.

She dashed into the house, to return in a moment tying a wide brimmed hat under her chin. She had put on a big coat of the old-fashioned 'ulster' style, and carried a basket of eggs and butter. They were soon on the way back to the city, Charles Stewart following the car with his steady gallop.

Miss O'Connor's face was very grim when she entered Duke Percival's flat. To her it was humiliating beyond words that she should have to enter his abode. But when she stood beside Nora's bed, and looked down at the little white face, now lit up with joy at the sight of 'Aunt Delia' again, and saw two soft arms stretched towards her, she forgot all else save that here was Nora — her own little Nora, the child who had crept into her lonely old heart years ago and stayed there ever since. 'Me darling!' she cried, and gathered her into her arms.

And how they talked. And that in spite of the nurse who informed Miss O'Connor that the doctor wished the patient to have quietness, Aunt Delia soon 'ran' this well-meaning nurse, and they were left to themselves.

Nora felt as happy as a child. She had but one regret — that she could not tell her aunt the truth that she was married. How she yearned to be free to say to her, 'you need not be ashamed of me — I am Mrs Duke Percival.' If only Duke had written before he had been wounded and taken prisoner! But now, perhaps, she would never hear from him again.

She begged her aunt not to ask any questions — she could tell her nothing at present. Later perhaps there was a secret which might surprise her!

Miss O'Connor, only too glad to have the girl back again at any price, told her not to worry. But she was determined not to allow her to remain under the roof of Duke Percival a day longer than was necessary. From her point of view, it was, of course, a scandalous state of affairs that Nora should be in his house at all.

The doctor, calling later, pronounced her much better, and said, much to Aunt Delia's satisfaction, that the nurse's services could be dispensed with.

It was settled also that as soon as ever Nora was well enough, she should go to Mount Rosemary, and there remain for as long as she wished.

The next morning Miss O'Connor said that she was going over to Rathgar, to let Harry and Julia know. 'They have been so terribly anxious about you,' she added, as Nora said nothing. 'I believe it has added years to Harry's age.'

'He deserved to suffer,' replied Nora, so bitterly that her aunt was astonished. 'I can never forgive them for what they have done! It was they who separated me from my — from Duke.'

'But girl, dear! What else would they do? I advised them the same way, too. Unfortunately they were too late; the mischief was done. Well — well! We will say no more about it now. But don't let you blame your brother or Julia — all they did was for the best.'

And Nora, feeling that as they did not know the truth of her relations with Duke they could not be blamed for acting as they had done, said no more. But she begged that they might not come to see her until she was at Mount Rosemary; and to this Aunt Delia agreed. Then she set off with her great news, leaving Nora with Charles Stewart for company. The dog's joy had been very great. At first he seemed hardly able to believe that it was really Nora, his old playmate, who lay so quietly in bed; and he kept returning to look at her again and again. At the present moment his big head was pushed up near her pillow, and now and then he would give a little whimper and thrust his cold nose against her cheek, as if to say, 'please look at me — speak to me. Aren't you glad to see me again?'

And she would stoke his beautiful head and talk to him; telling him all her secrets; whispering to him what she could not have told to anyone else; and the great faithful collie with his eyes fixed lovingly on her face seemed to understand and sympathise with all she said. In the first week of April Nora went to Mount Rosemary.

17

BELOVED

And so in the house beloved of her childhood, with the everlasting hills around her, Nora awaited the coming of her child.

Pierre Lamont had several times been very near to breaking his solemn promise to his master; he was fairly sure that in the circumstances Monsieur himself would have wished him to do so, and that if he should return and discover all that Madame had been compelled to suffer, Pierre — to whom she had been left as a sacred charge — would come in for a hard time. But, on the other hand, Monsieur might have had some reason, unknown to Pierre, for still keeping the marriage secret. Therefore, after much perplexed thought, he decided to wait a while longer. Although no more news had come about Duke, there was still hope; if he was a wounded prisoner he might be exchanged and would then probably be allowed home. All this Pierre kept saying to Nora when he came out to see her about twice a week. He and Miss O'Connor were firm friends now; she even allowed him to cook some of his 'French concoctions' for Nora. Harry and Julia came to see her, too. They were both very loving and kind; but still Nora felt in the depths of her sensitive soul that there was a wall of misunderstanding between them and herself. None of them, not even Aunt Delia, who loved her so, could ever forget that she — whom they believed unmarried — was about to bring a child into the world who would have no name and no father. And Nora's attitude in regard to the coming of her child puzzled them not a little. Although seldom speaking of it, she did not hesitate to do so when necessary, and at times it seemed as if she was almost proud of it. They thought that was because she did not understand. And another thing which angered all of them was that she bought for it very beautiful and expensive things. And bought them, too, out of Duke's money, for he had left a large sum in the bank in Pierre's name, so that it could be used for Nora's benefit if she needed it at any time.

'That she should use that man's money, and I telling her that she could have all she wanted from us — my God! Julia, I can't understand her — can you?' cried Harry, furiously.

'No, I cannot,' said his wife. 'It must be that she simply does not understand what this will mean to her. Afterwards she will realise it, and then she will suffer, poor girl.'

As for Nora herself she was happy, in a strange self-contained way. She was about to bring Duke's child into the world, and this to her was a sacred and uplifting thought. Her anxiety about her husband and the fact that she could not reveal her marriage to those who loved her much, were her two great troubles at this time. She knew, and perfectly understood, the point of view of her own family, but she could not tell them the truth at present, and this left her so that only to Pierre could she speak freely about the little stranger who was so soon expected. Pierre, with all a true Frenchman's love of children, took an immense interest in all the preparations made for the child. All the dainty little garments were displayed to him, and he went into the requisite raptures over them, to Nora's delight, for no one else took any interest in them — except, perhaps, Charles Stewart, who sniffed at them in a puzzled way now and then. Aunt Delia, indeed, found herself one day unable to refrain from saying very bitterly, that 'the plainer such children were dressed the better for them.' For a moment Nora flushed painfully, but then she smiled queerly to herself and made no reply.

'I hope the girl's reason is not going,' thought Miss O'Connor rather uneasily as she turned and went into the house, leaving Nora sitting sewing in the porch, with the scent of the lilac and syringa all about her.

Aunt Delia's loving heart was sore within her, just

because she felt that she could not allow her love to go forth to greet this child of Nora's. How she longed to be able to do so. How she would, in other circumstances, have waited and watched for its arrival with loving anxiety. With what tender care she would have helped to fashion the little garments, whose only message to her now seemed to be one of shame and disgrace. But her love for Nora was very deep, and she would sit and talk to her by the hour, telling her of her own girlhood, but telling especially about Ireland — the trials and sorrows of dear 'Dark Rosaleen'. It was a subject of which the old rebel never tired, and Nora was glad to listen. Such talk took her away from her own troubles — made her forget her present anxieties. Yes, and awakened a very real love for her country in her heart. For the first time she began to think of these things and to be proud of her nationality; began, too, to be vaguely sorry that her husband was on England's side in the present war. So Miss O'Connor's ideals bore good fruits as Nora listened to her while the two sat in the garden in the twilight and watched the purpling shadows come down over the Dublin hills.

Nora's mind was also made up about the keeping of the oath. She was resolved that if Duke had not returned, or if there was no news of him within six months after the birth of her baby, she would reveal her marriage. She felt that for the sake of the child she must do so. Pierre had informed her of the death of Everard Percival, and she knew that in course of time, should her child be a boy he would be head of the House of Percival.

And in the first week of June, just as the sun was rising over the Dublin mountains, Duke's son was born. Nora, as she clasped the little rose-bud face close to her breast, touched with her other hand the silken bag in which was her wedding ring.

Pierre had been staying at Mount Rosemary for the past week, and he and Miss O'Connor were sitting together in the kitchen, listening to the nurse and doctor as they moved about in the little bedroom where Nora fought her battle with pain. It had seemed a long night, both were fagged and weary, when suddenly there came a sound that brought them both to their feet —t he shrill wailing cry of a little soul as it made its entry into this queer old world of ours.

They looked at one another and then both made the sign of the Cross.

'*Mon Dieu!*' cried Pierre, 'of a certainly it is the little one!'

'Glory be to God, but that's the baby at last!' murmured Aunt Delia.

To Nora the days of convalescence were very sweet. Her baby was such a wonder! There never had been such a baby before. Even the nurse admitted that; and Pierre, whose sister had six — a great family for a Frenchwoman — said that never, never had his eyes beheld a child of such beauty and such strength. He was a fine child certainly, as even Harry and Julia had to admit when they came out to see Nora. But they did not go into raptures over him. Harry, indeed, hardly troubled to conceal his dislike of the child.

'What are you going to call him?' asked Aunt Delia.

'You ought to put him under the protection of some saint who might help him through life — the poor little mite,' said Julia.

Nora flushed angrily as she looked at them standing there and pitying her baby! If they only knew!

'His name is to be Duke Everard,' she said; and nothing they could say — and they said much — could make her alter this decision. Indeed, she sent Pierre to the church for fear that they might not give the right names to the priest.

Nora recovered rapidly, and in a few weeks was out in the garden among the June roses, wheeling Duke Everard up and down its paths, as he lay in state in the most expensive baby car which Pierre could buy. And by its side, self-appointed escort and guard of honour, always walked Charles Stewart. He loved the baby, as is the way of his breed with children.

And all this time, unknown to Nora, Harry and Julia were trying to find what they considered would be a suitable home for the child —if possible away in the country with people of the decent peasant class.

***

In July of that year, a thin, haggard man with a beard of many weeks' growth, and red-brown eyes weary with pain and anxiety, found himself in Johannesburg, where he had been sent by the Boers, along with several other British prisoners, in exchange for certain Boer prisoners.

He was still weak from his wound, which had been long in healing, and he was generally feeling that in spite of his regained freedom, life was not worth living. He knew, too, that Jack Vane was dead. By a strange turn of Fate, the Boers, when taking Duke away as prisoner, had come across Vane's dead body as it lay on the veldt, and there Percival had looked his last on his beloved comrade. Thus he also knew that the letter to Nora, which he had given to Vane, could never reach her. Unshaven and ragged as he was, his first inquiry, after reporting at the British headquarters, was for letters — for news from home. And many letters were there for him; some of them had been there for months. He glanced at the envelopes only, until he came to Pierre's handwriting. He tore this open, and Nora's letter fell out—the one she had written on leaving Greystones. As he read it his face showed the various emotions through which he was passing — love, surprise, sorrow, remorse.

Again and again he read the loving words, the wistful appeal that he would release her from the oath, on account of the child. 'God forgive me', he breathed, 'but I never thought of that.'

Duke Percival had changed in many ways, and above all he had changed in a spiritual manner. The God whom he had doubted — whose very existence he had questioned — had spoken in no uncertain voice on the battle-field and in the prison camp; and Duke had learned to go upon his knees in pray and supplication as he had not done since he used to say the Lord's Prayer, at his mother's knee in Belmont.

He then read Pierre's letter, in which he described in vivid French the finding by chance of Madame — so lonely, so desolate; and how he had taken her to the flat. There was another letter from Pierre also, in which he said that Nora had gone to Mount Rosemary; but Nora herself had not again written.

The next letter he opened was from the family solicitors. They regretted to inform him that his father Sir Roger, was dead, and they intimated that if Duke could return to Ireland his presence at Belmont, as the present baronet, was very desirable. And then for the first time he noticed that the envelope had been addressed to —'Sir Duke Percival'.

It did not take him long to make arrangements to return home. Those in authority put no obstacles in his way when they heard his reasons, and a week later he crossed the gangway of the steamer which would bring him again to the shores of Ireland. Shaved and immaculately groomed and clothed again, he looked more like the Duke of other days; but he was much thinner and appeared older. He thought that the journey would never come to an end.

On a foolish, boyish impulse, he had not sent word that he was coming. He wanted to surprise Nora, and on reaching Dublin he left his luggage at the station—not indeed that he had much luggage left — and mounting an outside-car, directed the driver to take him to Mount Rosemary.

It was about half-past six on a beautiful summer evening when he reached Miss O'Connor's home. Its location was, of course, unknown to him, and the driver had been compelled to make inquiries along the road. But he drew up now at the gate of Mount Rosemary. 'I think this should be the place, sir,' he said.

And as he spoke Duke heard a laugh from within the gate, a girl's laugh that he had often heard in his dreams on the African veldt, and in the prison camp.

'Yes — this is the place,' he said, 'you need not wait,' and he threw the man a sovereign.

Opening the gate very quietly, he stole softly into the garden, and slipping behind a big rose bush he gazed his fill at the picture before him. Nora sat in the porch in a rocking-chair, the baby was on her lap, and she was talking — partly to him and partly to Charles Stewart. The latter was listening far more intently than the baby, who seemed rather bored, as babies often do. She was not much changed; a little thinner and paler, but the same lovely eyes, the same adorable smile.

Miss O'Connor came up the garden from the far end and called out — 'Your tea is ready, Nora — give the baby to Pierre'; and to Duke's amusement Pierre came forward and took the baby into his arms with every appearance of pride and delight. Nora stood talking to him for a minute, and then Harry and Julia who were spending the evening at Mount Rosemary, came out into the porch.

Nora was turning to enter the house, when Duke stepped forward and strode towards her. 'Nora!' he called — 'Nora!'

She stood and looked at him for a moment, deathly white. They thought she was going to faint, and Harry moved to her side, but she pushed him aside and with one great cry — 'Beloved!' she threw herself into the arms of her husband.

He kissed her mouth, her eyes, her hair, murmuring a thousand words of love; and she clung to him as if she could never let him go. Pierre, holding the baby tightly, had tears in his eyes; but the rest who were watching the scene, were at first speechless from sheer rage at what they regarded as Duke's shameless audacity.

Harry Connor was the first to recover. Striding over to where the two stood oblivious of all the world but just their own selves, he put his hand on Nora's shoulder.

'Come away from that man,' he cried, 'have you no self-respect — no decency left? And as for you — you cad — clear out of this before I horsewhip the very life out of you.'

But Duke did not move and took no notice of Harry's threat. Nora still clung to him, while Pierre, with the baby, was edging closer to his adored master.

'Do you hear?' foamed Harry — 'Leave the place; and leave my sister! Are you satisfied with what you have made her?'

'Yes — quite satisfied,' then answered Duke quietly.

Slipping an arm round Nora he went over to the porch where Aunt Delia and Julia stood trembling and whitefaced.

'Miss O'Connor,' he said, in the gallant manner which became him so well, 'I wish to thank you for the care which you have taken of my dear and honoured wife—Lady Percival.'

***

Of course, afterwards, Miss O'Connor affirmed that she always knew it! — as if anyone could ever think anything else of Nora. But all the same she gave the faithful Pierre 'a piece of her mind' for not speaking out.

Julia during the evening made frequent references to 'her ladyship,' which greatly annoyed Harry, who was feeling very small indeed. His wife added to his humiliation by saying, as she prepared the baby for bed, Nora being out in the garden still with Duke — 'and to imagine, Harry, that you were actually looking for a home in a cottage for this child! Why he will be Sir Duke Percival one day if he lives long enough. And even now he is the heir to Belmont...Do you hear that, you little weeney darling thing, you are the heir of Belmont.' But her husband had fled and heard no more.

Out in the peaceful garden, with the daylight dying, and the hundred and one perfumes of the flowers enveloping them, Duke held his girl wife in his arms and kissed the slim finger on which he had just slipped the wedding ring which was never more to leave it.

'Sweetheart, can you forgive me?' he asked.

Nora opened her sweet eyes in astonishment.

'Why, there is nothing to forgive, Beloved,' she said.